The Ethnic Cleansing of the English

The Ethnic Cleansing of the English

John Smith

authorHOUSE®

AuthorHouse™ UK
1663 Liberty Drive
Bloomington, IN 47403 USA
www.authorhouse.co.uk
Phone: 0800.197.4150

Published by AuthorHouse 05/14/2015

ISBN: 978-1-5049-4133-4 (sc)
ISBN: 978-1-5049-4134-1 (e)

Print information available on the last page.

Contents

Chapter 1

Whither little England?

In prehistoric times one may imagine Britain was populated by a band or bands of hunter gatherers who variously kept well away from their fellow's or rivals, we can only imagine fairly uncivilised times. The likelihood is that these 'groups' which almost certainly were based on family ties were competing for resources. These people the Neanderthals were a relatively primitive race. The latest theory is that they were 'displaced' by modern man around 50,000 years ago who it is thought originally came from Africa. Scientists can only speculate about this prehistory period but it is thought that modern man with his greater brainpower in competition with the Neanderthals eventually drove them into extinction. It is thought that this took place over a period that is admittedly uncertain but estimated to be between 500 and 5000 years.

Whether modern man originally came from Africa and whether in intervening periods they have been infused with 'foreign' blood is a matter whose relevance is a debate for another occasion. As far as one can tell however these people would also have been hunter gatherer types with their prowess derived from physical strength and a crude form of leadership used to determine who should lead or control the group or groups. This basic concept of control and power has not changed throughout the ages of man despite our current 'sophistication'. With increasing populations and limited resources man will continue to struggle with his 'fellow' man for resources forever it seems.

It appears that civilisation originally progressed slowly in most parts of the world with one or two exceptions. These anomalies, the Egyptians, some South American tribes and others are whilst fascinating in themselves, not the subject of this book.

Fast forward to 2000 years or so ago when the Roman military machine invaded and colonised Britain. The Roman military idea was based on high levels of discipline; to govern by military force if persuasion or coercion was unsuccessful. There were arguably many benefits to Roman occupation throughout the mediterranean area and in Britain including the introduction of mortar and concrete, a primitive form of law, record-keeping, administration, advanced construction and civil order – pax Romana.

Concrete was arguably the greatest invention of the Romans who in some other respects were not creative or inventive and relied heavily on the early work of the Greeks. Had the Romans been more inventive and capable of controlling their vast empire it is highly possible we would all still be under Roman rule today. Many Britons joined in with the inevitable and benefited from trade and interaction with their conquerors. Who is to say therefore that the influx and influence of the Romans was not in the long-term benefit of the people of Britain. This idea is of course highly relevant today but it takes no account of the perceived right to self-determination of an independent people. Who is to say that greater progress could not have been made without the invasion of this foreign military power; which when it left Britain in around 410 A.D left a power vacuum and a civilisation void. The void in Britain was of course subsequently filled by various tribes noted for their raping and pillaging qualities with the Vikings splitting the country into two creating the North East, South West divide, the Danelaw; then came the Anglo-Saxon conquest and subsequently the Normans.

1000 years ago the country was again conquered at the battle of Hastings by the Normans. The Normans were also the Norsemen from Scandinavia, our old 'friends' the pillaging and raping Vikings. Lead by the Duke of Normandy William (the bastard); who it is said had issues about the sovereignty of England with the then would be leader Harold. The conquerors raped and pillaged the lands of England and terrorised the population. Nearly all Anglo-Saxon landowners were dispossessed of their lands and property distributed amongst the conqueror's barons. Vast amounts of land in England remains under control of the descendants of William who with an army of a few thousand men changed the face of England forever.

It is undoubtedly the case that William was vicious but nonetheless a good administrator. He catalogued all of England's lands and chattels and effectively lay claim to all of it. He bestowed upon the church great wealth and upon his barons great power. Englishmen were obliged speak in Latin or French which was the official language of England for 200 years. We should not feel too badly about this because William had also conquered a lot of southern Italy, Sicily and much more.

England then entered a mediaeval period during which successive monarchs reigned supremely over the population with absolute power. This absolute power meant the power of life and death over all their subjects. It is little wonder therefore that the population became highly political in terms of its own survival and then for most survival was a matter of keeping one's head down, rather than having it chopped off. A docile and compliant population in the making?

England saw the last of its fighting mediaeval kings with Richard 111 who was defeated at the Battle of Bosworth. His skeleton has subsequently been exhumed and examined in detail having been found under a municipal car park in the East Midlands. Richard 111 was it appears another French Plantagenet 'Royal' whose lineage may cast doubt on the current monarch.

Few politicians wish to acknowledge the fact that England has been invaded several times and conquered in 1688 by William of Orange who also subsequently became Britain's monarch. This Dutch Protestant king being one of many foreign heads of state ruling in Britain over the course of the country's history.

We can move on to more modern times and review the demise of large sections of the population in the first and second world Wars. In the 1914/18 war, the so-called great War; almost a million young men, many volunteers; were sent to their deaths by officers who knew little and cared less about the value of their subordinates other than as cannon fodder. It may be more appropriate to describe these men as machine gun fodder since we are all familiar with the naive volunteer going 'over the top' into battle. It appears the commander of these poor arguably foolish men many of which were volunteers had no concept of the power of the machine gun and the concept of crossfire in open countryside.

These brave but naive volunteers gave their lives gladly it appears for the good of their country when called to arms by Kitchener. In 2014, 100 years after the commencement of this 'great war' Britain remembers the casualties and the massive impact the loss of so many men had both on the country and families. How did this occur you may well ask, why of course it was a result of the assassination of the

Archduke Ferdinand of Austria! This assassination led to the commencement of the war by the Germans and in particular their leader the Kaiser who it is thought with hindsight was power mad and somewhat mentally unbalanced.

In the Second World War millions of men on all sides were sent to their deaths in the interest of territory and political power. Most readers will recall the traditional view of this conflict in which Hitler invaded Poland with whom Britain had a treaty, despite assurances given to Neville Chamberlain the then Prime Minister of Britain. The great war leader Churchill it is said stepped in to rescue the nation and thanks to the RAF it appears prevented an invasion. America joined the war eventually after the bombing of Pearl Harbour and the rest is history.

A less popular view is that Hitler had no intention of invading Britain but following Churchill's disastrous military campaigns elsewhere eg, Gallipoli, Churchill continued to seek action in order to measure up to his great hero the Duke of Marlborough whom he had written about extensively. Men were sent to their deaths of course not just by their generals and senior officers but by the masters of the military; those elected politicians who had taken the place of the sovereigns under the guise of the Royal prerogative.

The ideas developed here it should be emphasised are not strict political analysis or comprehensive historical facts. This is not a problem since it is a personal view as valid as any other with which many will agree with and with which many will disagree. It is not the author's intention to seek consensus but to stimulate discussion and appropriate action. The reader may want to give consideration to Darwin's theory in relation to the development of populations and their ascendancy or otherwise. Darwin's theory, the survival of the fittest; does appear to break down in relation to socialist political systems and benefit based societies rightly or wrongly.

There are many difficulties within Britain ranging from the economy, the issue of mass immigration, religion etc, the list goes on. In order to suggest solutions it is first necessary to identify some of these problems in more detail. Britons live in a country described as a liberal modern Western democracy by many. Is this a proper analysis? Are we really a democracy? Is Britain still a two-party state, an elected dictatorship?

In the two world wars Germany was deemed universally to be the aggressor, later joined by Japan and Italy. They were finally defeated by the Allied forces of America, Britain and Russia. After the Second World War it is universally agreed that Britain was on its knees. Its young men were savagely reduced in number. Rationing continued for many years after the war and the population was whilst exuberant very tired of it all.

In due course the country began to recover and in 1956 the then Prime Minister Harold Macmillan declared the population had 'never had it so good'. Then came the swinging 60s when the population began to experience a degree of freedom of thought and imagination. They had 'free love', mods and rockers, and the advent of spaceflight.

Following the war as we all know the Windrush brought many immigrants to the shores of Britain said to compensate it is alleged for the manpower lost during the Second World War. Great resentment of these fresh 'invaders' was seen on the streets and there is still resentment over mass immigration which continues unabated today. It remained a mystery in 2013 when after Britain and America declared 'war on terror' in 2001, invaded Iraq and subsequently Afghanistan, both Muslim countries why given the circumstances Britain has allowed 2,000,000+ members of the Islamic community to settle in Britain. This is extraordinarily inconsistent and incomprehensible with many believing they are the enemy within. British forces remained in Afghanistan despite there being many deaths some of which arose from the hands of those the coalition sought to introduce democracy to. The days of British imperialism or a belief in it are clearly not over.

Chapter 2

Identity & Culture

Well what is the identity and culture of the British people? Is it their deep rooted history abundant in scientific discovery, engineering genius, enterprise, great statesmanship, music, cricket or what? Well perhaps not cricket. The traditional English person is quite easy going, mild and compliant but with a streak of defiance when aroused. It has to be said that the average English person is not apparently well educated, indeed there appears amongst the white working classes to be an insubordinate form of resistance to education. This is quite inexplicable but appears to stem from a perverse idea of masculinity. Many of us are 'young' enough to remember the 'swats' at school. Swats were people who preferred their books and 'slide rules' yes slide rules rather than playing football and cricket outside. The swats were derided as being somehow effeminate or peculiar.

But does the English personality have a dark side? We have seen corrupt politicians, supposedly they who set standards for the populace to follow. Since the exposure of Neil Hamilton some years ago in the cash for questions scandal many more politicians have been gradually exposed for being by and large corrupt liars interested only in themselves. The Daily Telegraph having obtained copies of MPs expenses set about exposing the cheating MPs as fiddlers and fraudsters. We have seen MPs and members of the upper house the Lords being sent to prison in recent years in relation to fraudulent expenses claims.

The pillar of our broadcasting establishment the BBC had it appears been harbouring a serial sex pest and molester for almost 50 years. 'Sir' Jimmy Savile had it appears been molesting young children and disabled folks for decades undetected or overlooked by the establishment. He was knighted and became firmly fixed within the establishment to be seen in public with the then prime minister Margaret Thatcher and escaping detection until after his death. More recently in the first days of May 2013 we saw William Roache, star of Coronation Street for over 45 years being charged with two counts of rape in relation to young ladies; being subsequently acquitted. We saw Stuart Hall ex-BBC presenter after vigorously protesting his innocence admitting to 14 counts of indecent assault many years ago. There is clearly something about the culture at the BBC, funded by the taxpayer; that requires serious investigation.

On 7 May 2013 Nigel Kennedy said he was appalled to hear the breaking story about further allegations of sex abuse of pupils by teachers at numerous music schools who appear to take pupils under their wings and abuse their positions to touch them sexually or worse. In one case a lady committed suicide after going through the ordeal of recalling the events in court.

On 28 May 2013 we saw Max Clifford, not BBC; a self-styled publicist pleading not guilty to 11 charges of assault made by seven different individuals. Again these charges being related to alleged conduct many years before. Clifford was accompanied by his wife, no doubt to her dying embarrassment: to be tried in Southwark Crown Court in June 2013.

We have often heard that the English do not care much for sex and certainly do not discuss it openly or with ease. It does appear however that the English attitude to sex is rather like certain members of the Catholic Church, clandestine, furtive, dirty and of course illegal. We do appear to have our fair share of pervert's in apparently very high places as well as low.

What strange perversion compels a man to abduct, molest and murder a little girl in Wales? In May 2013 Mark Bridger was tried for the abduction and the murder of young April Jones to the horror of the local community, the country and the world at large.

In June 2014 we see Rolf Harris; an Australian adopted by the English as a rather lovable if not talented figure: found guilty of numerous counts of sexual assault and sentenced to 8 years in prison. Throughout the trial he protested his innocence to charges which included sexual activity with his then young daughter's best friend.

Of course all societies have their pervert's, miscreants and criminals. The great distinguishing factor in Britain is however the apparent front, the facade of respectability that these notable persons portray until caught. Is hypocrisy a national characteristic? The bluff, the bluster it often turns to dust when they are charged. We must ask ourselves how this has come about? How such arrogance has apparently been encouraged?

We could do a statistical analysis and compare the relative crime rates for different crimes in different countries. Would this be of use, probably not. Even the U.K.'s criminal records statistical gathering is subject to certain vagaries and to attempt to compare different countries statistics would be to confuse apples and pears. What we can say as a 'civilised' society these sorts of crimes are totally unacceptable.

Whilst it is possible to make some general comments and analysis it is not possible to explain strange and perverse behaviour. For many the hymn 'Jerusalem' words by William Blake and musical arrangement by Sir Hubert Parry typifies all that is British and indeed English. The words include "…. until we have built Jerusalem in England's green and pleasant land …". This hymn takes on the appearance of what is good, wholesome and patriotic. It is indeed a stirring melody. It is arguably however quite perverse.

Jerusalem as we are all aware is the site of much conflict, death, raping and pillaging over the centuries. It is a religious site claimed to be sacred to Christians, Jews and Muslims alike. Perhaps this perverse view by some of the population of Britain is a function of their apparent brainwashing over the years by politicians and the BBC? Perhaps by way of perverse analysis it explains why there are now approximately 2,000,000+ Muslim worshippers in Britain? Many of these latter worshippers being committed entirely to the establishment of a Muslim caliphate in Britain although of course the so-called Muslim 'community' leaders contend that the majority of their fellow believers are perfectly reasonable law-abiding citizens. Does this view hold for those who have left Britain to fight Jihad?

When government abandons people, people abandon themselves and/or then revolt? We may take small comfort in the fact that those politicians who despise the people will eventually be overthrown, but overthrown by whom?

The Chilcott Enquiry and report into the Iraq war is long overdue and it is said has been deliberately sabotaged possibly to protect the former Prime Minister Blair. The public position stated is that there are difficulties in relation to concealing state secrets contained within the report. How many millions were spent on this public enquiry?

There are many aspects to the English culture, too numerous to mention; what we can be sure of is that it is rich, complex and some of it is dying out through either natural or unnatural causes. 'Proper' words are being replaced in English dictionaries through lack of use to be replaced by what appears to be slang. We see in the news on 12 August 2014 that after some 200 years the great British pub is in danger of extinction. Originally derived from inns or coaching houses set up along the stagecoach routes of the first postal delivery system in Dick Turpin's days we now see 31 pubs per week are closing. Whilst this may not be especially important and may simply be a matter of evolution (Darwin's theory?), the pub's principal cause of demise appears to be the availability of cheap booze at supermarkets, the growing non alcohol consuming part of the population and the risks associated with drink-driving; it is nonetheless highly symbolic of a change of culture.

For those of us watching the news in the middle of August 2014 and not wishing to be embarrassed by the performance of the England football or cricket teams we see the news announcing a new exciting player in the English cricket team. This player is of course Moeen Ali sporting a large Islamic style beard? We shall no doubt see this player repeatedly described as 'English' in due course as a result of the sloppy use of the English language by broadcasters. A football or cricket player in the England team is not necessarily English any more than an English person born in India is not Chinese.

On 22 August 2014 we see Malcolm Mackay an eminent football manager forced by notions of political correctness to make a grovelling apology for his allegedly racist remarks apparently contained in mobile telephone texts. The spectacle is reminiscent of confessions under McArthyism or obtained by torture in the Inquisition.

On the same day Channel 4 news reports on asylum seekers in various immigration centres being obliged to work for £1 per hour. The emphasis of the report is to encourage sympathy for asylum seekers who are reported as being exploited by unscrupulous authorities at the detention centre. A later report depicts the plight of the circumstances brought about by and upon themselves. Little thought or concern is given to the possibility that those who are allowed to stay eventually may turn on their hosts.

And so we see a docile, compliant, easy going indigenous population. It is abundantly clear that this laissez-faire attitude to everything but football is a large part of the problem, if of course in such a society there can be a problem or problems where they are encouraged to believe that all is normal and any person harbouring racist feelings is bad. Same-sex marriages are being celebrated in a society where every aspect of life, behaviour and beliefs is manipulated and constructed to maximise votes for the popular political parties. Even the word of God is compromised with the concept of marriage being 'tuned' to meet the wider needs of a minority population. The ascendancy and pre-eminent interests of the minority have effectively overturned the interests of the majority who gladly subscribe to their political 'masters' beliefs in the absence of their own considered views.

Chapter 3

Romanticism and Conflict

If we look back 100 years to the commencement of the First World War we noted that this is said to have started because of the assassination of the Archduke Ferdinand of Austria by Gavrilo Princip in Sarajevo. An additional ingredient is said to have been the rather strange behaviour of the German Kaiser, a man it is said who suffered from mental problems. It began in 1914 when German troops marched into Belgium. They then set about raping, killing and pillaging from the local population.

British men were called to arms on a voluntary basis through the medium of posters and propaganda stating that 'their country needs them'. This poster featuring Kitchener had a substantial effect in recruiting young men. Many men volunteered into the ranks and they included many underage boys. It became clear that they were very patriotic and saw this exploit as an adventure. Many with hindsight were very brave and many naive. There was also a great deal of peer pressure and anyone who didn't volunteer felt some pressure to join up.

It also became clear as the war wore on that the deployment of the machine gun was to take a dreadful toll on these men who walked or jogged into battle, an approach inappropriate and reminiscent of the 18th century approach to warfare. They were of course mown down in their thousands. This 'great war' or 'war to end all wars' as it was variously called took the lives of millions of young men. The consequences of this war live on to this day with many communities and families still only too aware of the dreadful cost of this ridiculous and pointless war.

Can we derive from this experience that the power vested in politicians is often dangerous to those who vest it and they in whom power is vested are often incompetent and thoughtless. Democracy, the least worst option?

On 8 August 2014 Britain and Europe commemorated the dead from the first world war. Many re-enactment's taking place and films produced especially for the occasion about the horrors of trench warfare and the effectiveness of early machine guns. We see depictions of British soldiers fighting bravely at Mons at the commencement of the First World War against overwhelming odds. No one can doubt their bravery and sacrifice and many Victoria crosses were awarded, many posthumously. We are obliged if only for objectivities sake nonetheless to question the need for their sacrifice and the numbers involved. We must ask 'was it worth it' as many no doubt did at the time. Then of course we must ask the same question after the Second World War.

The UK and Commonwealth sent 9 million combatants to war in the First World War. 8 million returned many of whom received life changing injuries.

The Second World War.

The Second World War was brought about from the United Kingdom point review of view by Adolf Hitler invading Poland with whom England had a treaty. Neville Chamberlain the then Prime Minister asserted that he had seen Herr Hitler and had agreed peaceful terms with him.

Winston Churchill then came to power and took England to war with Germany. Many take the view that Winston Churchill was not the hero that propaganda suggests but that he was a warmonger with a number of previously failed disastrous exploits to his credit.

Again men volunteered as well as the conscripts in the war which levied a heavy price on the British population. The country won the war on the battleground, eventually with America's help; to find itself bankrupt at the end of it. Wartime rationing lasted until well after the war with the Britain victorious but on its knees.

It is notable that the large military contingent of the British Army of the Rhine stationed in Germany since the Second World War was to be withdrawn in the next few years according to an announcement made in 2013. The ending of this expensive occupation being long overdue.

911 and the third world war.

For years the rise of Islamism has been characterised by kidnappings, hostage taking, hijacks, bomb attacks and suicide bombers.

On 11 September 2001 a number of aircraft were hijacked in the United States and two of them flown into the two high rise towers of the World Trade Centre in New York amongst other targets. It is estimated that around 3000 people perished in those attacks on the same day and it appears safe to suggest that the world has never been the same since. Innocent people going about their business were slaughtered by Islamic terrorists who carried out the attacks in the name of the prophet Muhammad and God. What motivates these people to do such terrible things?

God only knows? It appears there is deep resentment within the Islamic 'religious' population in relation to the West's interest in what they claim to be their lands. This includes of course the invasions of Iraq and Afghanistan. A simpler answer suggests that Islam is an aggressive and intolerant ideology.

We have seen suicide bombings in London and it appears many other attempts at causing serious casualties by terror throughout the world have been averted. Some have not. No one can doubt the fervour of the suicide bomber who is prepared to die for his cause in the belief they will become a martyr. Many argue that such levels of commitment can only be combated with equal terror! It is believed with that in mind that George W Bush launched the war on terror in Iraq with the bombing of Baghdad under his 'shock and awe' campaign but was Iraq the real problem?

Few can doubt that the Third World War has been ongoing for some time but because it is being dubbed an asymmetric war it has not been formally declared by any of the participants despite the fact that it commenced in earnest on '911'. Although no war has been formally declared hostilities are clearly ongoing. It is also evident that there are few great battles and few clear demarcation lines. What can reasonably be said however is that there is a battle of ideas, a battle of cultures, a clash of civilisations.

Many people in the West and in particular Europe have complained bitterly about the 'Islamification' of their cultures. This is particularly so in some Scandinavian countries and in Britain where the policies of mass immigration are seeing millions of people of the Islamic persuasion settle together with their families, extended and otherwise.

On 15 April 2013 the Boston Marathon was subjected to 2 bombs killing three people who were spectators and injuring over 140. This took place in the crowded streets of Boston and it was evident from the press coverage that the bombs had been placed within the spectator areas in order to make the maximum impact and to create the most chaos through the medium of terror as was possible.

This event being immediately preceded in the UK by four Islamic men from Luton, so-called British people; being convicted of planning to blow up various targets in the UK. One of these targets being a territorial Army base which they had intended to attack by attaching a bomb to a small radio controlled toy sent under the gates of the local territorial Army base. Remember Norman Tebbit's much derided cricket test?

In the third week of September 2013 a group claiming to be members of Al Shebab killed dozens of people in a shopping mall in Africa after asking people if they were 'believers'; those that claimed to be believers were released, those that did not were shot. There is little doubt with that and more recent events that a religious war is ongoing. The killers during their shooting spree stopped to pray to their God. A God which is apparently inspiring such evil acts.

In 2014 we see the war continuing in Syria and Iraq and a group called 'ISIS' have now proclaimed an Islamic state, a caliphate; in large tracts of northern Syria and Iraq.

American and UK airports report a higher security alert than previously in July 2014 as a result of intelligence that suggests that terrorist bombs may be concealed in uncharged electronic devices. Passengers are therefore being advised to ensure that their laptops and mobile phones etc are fully charged prior to embarkation so that security checks may ascertain whether the devices can operate as the devices they purport to be.

On 23 June 2014 sky news reported an interview with Khalid Mahmood an MP in Birmingham who stated that it was his belief that more than 400 'British' citizens were fighting in either Syria or Iraq as insurgents. The great fear being in the UK that these insurgents may return to the UK, as indeed they are entitled to do, to capitalise on their fighting activities and skills to disrupt the UK. The estimate is later raised to the thousands. On the same day BBC News reveals the identity of a third Briton from Aberdeen in addition to two cited from Wales, performing in a Jihad video broadcast on the Internet. In the same news bulletin there are reports of 20 far right extremists said to be from Poland/Eastern Europe attacking people attending a music festival in North London.

In August 2014 we see the news broadcasting the death of an American news reporter James Foley. Foley had previously been captured by Islamic fighters and apart from being American had it appears no reason to be punished; he suffered beheading. The execution was carried out and broadcast on social media for all to see. That is to say all except those who experienced the self censorship of the mainstream news media. It appears the executioner 'Jihadi John' was 'British'! It further appears that the strategy of the now self-proclaimed Islamic state fighters is to consolidate the Islamic state caliphate in Syria and Iraq.

The Iraq war.

There were many people completely opposed to the war in Iraq and this was clear from a march of around 1 million protesters in London at the time of the commencement of the conflict. It appears that Prime Minister Blair and the then President of the United States George W Bush had decided that Iraq had weapons of mass destruction (WMD), apparently contrary to the intelligence which it was believed in any event had been 'sexed up' to provide a pretext so that they could invade the country. It was decided that this would be done on the basis of shock and awe and inevitably the Iraq army collapsed and fled.

Despite the efforts of Hans Blix and his team of investigators no WMD could be found. Saddam Hussein the so-called dictator of Iraq at the time fled and was later found hiding underground in what can best be described as a hole in the ground. He was tried by his countrymen and hanged. Since these events the country has descended into anarchy which continues today. It is helpful to define anarchy for this purpose and in the case of Iraq it means civil war in a country without effective government and includes numerous substantial suicide bombs on an ongoing day-to-day basis.

It must be evident to all that the country has all but been destroyed and what remains is in a state of chaos. This is notwithstanding the billions of pounds and dollars spent in this somewhat perplexing warfare. It is difficult to see what has been achieved except the possible enrichment of certain arms companies despite the stated aim including within it a desire to introduce Western democracy to Iraq. Such arrogance? Despite Saddam Hussein's 'style' there was at least relative stability.

In the middle of June 2014 we see 'ISIS' taking control of a further number of towns in Syria and Iraq. They are spreading a particularly unpleasant version of Islam and carrying out the summary execution of their opponents many of whom are of different Islamic persuasions as they progress and systematically terrorise the country. We note that Mr Blair the former British Prime Minister eloquently if not misguidedly states that this continuing terrorist insurgency has nothing to do with the invasion of Iraq in 2003 by him and George W Bush. Mr Blair advocates troops be sent back to Iraq to take control of the situation.

Some have described Mr Blair as a misguided, zealous, religious warmonger and that had Saddam Hussein remained in control in Iraq then at least there would have been some stability. It appears that a combination of George W Bush and Mr Blair's religious fervour coupled with a willingness to read into intelligence reports what they wanted to see has brought us all in the West to the brink of a very dark abyss the bottom of which we see later.

In August 2014 we see that the self-proclaimed Islamic state in Syria and Iraq is terrorising a tribal group, the Yazidis; in Kurdistan. With the fragmentation of Iraq, its armed forces and its government in disarray; the United States and Britain are again drawn into expensive supporting actions in this troubled part of the Middle East. The conflict in Iraq is clearly a part of a wider conflict Islamic East v West which can now reasonably be called the Third World war.

The war in Afghanistan.

It is interesting to note that the war in Afghanistan was commenced with the full knowledge that historically the British had previously failed in the country and that only a few years before the might of the Russian army was also humiliated and kicked out of the country by the Taliban. Is it any surprise therefore that the Americans and the British had become bogged down in Afghanistan with dozens of deaths and little if anything to show for it. The billions the war has cost cannot be said to be anything like a reasonable expenditure in relation to the outcome. It appears that the Americans realised this and were committed to removing their troops from the country by 2014/5. In similar fashion it appears the British handed over the security of the country back to the Taliban since the Afghan army appears to be corrupt, ineffective and incompetent.

As a result of the conflicts in Iraq and Afghanistan Tony Blair was obliged to give evidence at an enquiry into the war in Iraq. He was also rewarded for his efforts by being appointed peace envoy to the Middle East by the so-called Quartet. He's been highly rewarded for his work despite the Middle East itself descending into an apparent perpetual turmoil. In July 2014 we see Palestine and Israel at war and calls for Mr Blair's resignation as peace envoy.

The Afghans are themselves obliged to manage and police their own country. This follows years of bloodshed and the deaths and disfigurement of many coalition troops including British soldiers. The insurgents as they are called became proficient in IED's (Improvised explosive devices) and many troops had their legs and various other body parts blown off as a result of the skill and determination of the locals who continue to reject imperialist ideas.

The Afghans themselves are a ragbag of tribesman and tribal members occupying villages often without the most basic facilities. They are invariably illiterate. The Taliban themselves invoke Sharia law upon the population but it is important to realise that there is no discrete demarcation that one can draw between the general population and the Taliban since they are often one and the same. The Afghan army also drawn from this largely illiterate population, many of whom are engaged in the production of opium poppies, they are an undisciplined corrupt armed force often consumers of their own opium or marijuana products.

At the beginning of May 2013 we saw three brave British soldiers blown up in the newly provided so called armoured vehicles provided somewhat late in the conflict to protect the occupants. These three young men died leaving grieving families but for what? We were told that the war in both Iraq and Afghanistan were intended to quell the possibility of terrorism occurring in the UK. Better to fight them in their own backyard? This ludicrous policy has achieved nothing as we have seen elsewhere to prevent so called home grown British terrorists plotting terror and carrying out what appear to be revenge acts within the UK. Is it too much common sense to suggest that these brave soldiers if deployed anywhere should be deployed in the UK to protect their homeland?

In October 2013 we saw that a coroner's court records a verdict of unlawful killing in relation to 6 servicemen that were blown up in a Scorpion armoured vehicle in Afghanistan. The youngest of the six being 19 years old.

Chapter 4

The Special Relationship/s

What exactly does this mean? This apparently refers to an alleged special relationship with the United States principally stemming from cooperation in the Second World War and prior to that our historical connections with this former British colony.

Britain once had a special relationship with the United States of America without doubt. This was 200 years ago before they kicked us out of America; today we are a small island off the coast of Europe apparently in terminal decline. The economy, currently the sixth largest in the world is in real terms stagnant at best. Whilst much of Europe and the United States are also suffering from stagnation Britain's problems whilst not entirely unique do place a set of large arguably insuperable burdens on its ability to recover.

We see the United States a dominant financial powerhouse of the world and the greatest military power exerting its muscle here and there from time to time. The British are seen to be the United States greatest ally. This is however, often interpreted as the British providing support to the United States when called upon to do so. Examples are of course Iraq and Afghanistan. The special relationship didn't stop the United States invading Guyana in 1983 without reference to the UK the former colonial power, when acting in its own best interest. Ronald Reagan attempted to explain the 'secrecy' as 'need to know' and the US certainly wanted to ensure secrecy since the UK may have objected. The special relationship was also cast aside in the early days of the Falklands conflict when the United States initially declined to give even diplomatic support to Britain because of its own commercial interests in South America.

There is no doubt that there is a form of special relationship that Britain enjoys with its 'big brother'. There is little doubt that the sharing of high-level security information and intelligence does now occur. This is because unlike certain other countries, e.g. France, there is a high level of confidentiality and mutual trust between the parties. The extradition treaty however gives much cause for concern with UK authorities apparently being much readier to extradite alleged offenders to the USA than the USA itself would itself.

Europe, the Euro, democracy.

Europe, the socialist bloc.

In the days of Jacques Delors and the formation of the current EU we can easily identify and recognise the tendency to socialism. The desire to share, the desire to be 'fair', the desire to redistribute, the desire to make everyone equal and be the same; except of course the unelected leaders of the EU. Who can doubt from this latest model of socialism that the model is fatally flawed and destined to fail?

During the early part of 2014 we see much discussion amongst the political classes and the media in relation to Europe and the free movement of goods and services and workers. There appears to be little understanding amongst British 'leaders' about the implications of these simple principles now enshrined in various EU treaties. Perhaps Britain should introduce a system to make it obligatory for any politician standing for election that they be tested on their knowledge of matters they are likely to be asked to consider on our behalf.

In Spain in early 2014 we see a country struggling to emerge from deep financial difficulties. With 25% youth unemployment and huge amounts of unsold property it is difficult to see Spain emerging any time soon from its current problems. We note that Italy, Cyprus, France and Greece are struggling with severe budget deficits, the latter being rife with social unrest. Who can doubt with even the slightest knowledge of the problem that it is rooted in socialism? Charles Dickens knew and every housewife knows if you spend more than you earn there will be serious <u>difficulties</u>.

Mr Cameron a British Prime Minister vowed to try and renegotiate the British deal in Europe. Fat chance the member states replied, politely! It is evident that politicians lack an understanding of the nature of the treaties entered into in relation to Europe and the member states and more particularly that the free movement of people is a precept, a pillar of the European state itself. To suggest that treaties can be renegotiated against the interests of a majority of other EU member states is pie in the sky or something more alarming. In June 2014 it became evident that most member states have no intention of supporting Mr Cameron's position therefore one must conclude that he was simply biding his time until the next election and hoping to play the electorate for idiots once more. Remember his 'no ifs, no buts' promise on immigration?

On 9 June 2014 at the EU summit the topics included a discussion about the next head of the EU Commission the strong favourite being the former Prime Minister of Belgium Jean-Claude Juncker who Mr Cameron opposed.

Mr Cameron referred to the undemocratic selection process for the next head of the EU commission and still believes he can influence the EU and renegotiate terms for the UK by 2017, or does he? Who is he kidding? This self-delusion and propaganda is dangerous. Is it not about time the country elected politicians who had some knowledge of the affairs of the country, some idea of integrity and practicality? 2017 is of course the date from which Mr Cameron promised an in/out referendum on Europe for the British people. This assumed of course that he was in a position to do so in 2017. Who got us into this mess in the first place?

In the first half of 2014 many had noticed that Prime Minister Cameron continued to play his bluff hand of politics in relation to the new EU Commissioner, the need for change within the EU etc etc. Any observer who may have taken the time out to study the structure of the EU will realise that the founding 'pillars' as they are known i.e., the free movement of goods, services and people etc are realistically not negotiable since they are the precepts on which the whole EU edifice is founded. Mr Cameron is either very ignorant or attempting to mislead the population of the UK by suggesting that he can renegotiate terms with the EU.

BBC Newsnight on 23 June 2014 reported that the Polish Foreign Minister Sikorsky had been overheard berating Prime Minister Cameron and referring to him as 'stupid' if he thinks he can make any serious changes to the appointment of the proposed new head of the EU commission Mr Juncker. This outburst was very embarrassing even to many Polish people despite it probably being a case of hitting the 'nail' squarely on the head.

It would have been easily possible to use most of this work to analyse the problems of the Eurozone and the incompatibility of the states within it. The northern industrial states and the southern European sunny states like Spain and Portugal being at best strange 'bedfellows'. From the commercial collapse and social unrest of Greece to the triple dip economic recession of Italy in 2014 to the small but positive growth of the United States and the UK. Even the powerhouse of Germany is weighed down by the 'sea' anchor of this socialist bloc in 2014 showing a stagnant economic performance. The Germans it appears are seeing the disadvantages of such a bloc where sovereignty is pooled.

The Euro.

This is a currency adopted by 17 of the 27 nations of the EU. It is a currency which was surprisingly adopted by many countries who apparently gave little or no thought to the impact on their sovereignty or democracy that such an arrangement would inevitably bring. The Germans and their beloved Deutschmark is a particular case in point. Whilst the Germans were able to meet the appropriate tests set out for membership of the Euro currency many less industrious nations were not and this is clearly causing the current strains, eg Greece. These 'strains' were inevitable, throughout the history of the Eurozone when less productive countries strayed from the agreed constraints then European politicians previously allowed this to go unchallenged. Let us not be too smug about this the pound is the result of a European currency bloc introduced by the Romans 2000 years or so ago in Britain.

Noting that for the past two years the Eurozone economy has been stagnant despite tweaks to the interest rate by the European Central bank and the steadily increasing value of the pound the Euro declining to 81p in value in early 2014 and continued down subsequently.

Countries nonetheless still clamour to join the euro the next deadline being in 2015. Countries queuing up to join are of course former satellites of the Soviet union who see security and protection for themselves by joining the Euro states. This of course brings wider questions into consideration as Russia masses its troops along its border with Ukraine, feeling itself to be threatened by the Euro states. Is Turkey a broadly Islamic state in Europe, should it be allowed to join?

Democracy in Europe.

Western democracy is held up to be a great example by way of its achievements. It is a fact however that the EU is run largely by an army of unelected officials. The commission is not elected by the people but by politicians.

Most governments are of course elected by a minority of people and as such this raises questions about the efficacy and legitimacy of many Western governments. Should there be a minimum simple majority obligation in relation to the legitimacy of power held by any government?

On 13 May 2014 Channel 4 news broadcast an informative piece which in summary reported that the European Court of Justice had ruled that Google must remove allegedly old but accurate information published about a Spanish individual who had applied to the said court. There was no suggestion that the information published on the web was inaccurate or mischievous but that it contained information which was no longer a current relevant topic. This is quite extraordinary and appears to contradict a further European legal precept. The right to freedom of speech and expression. For a European court to oblige Google to remove a published item about an individual is to effectively rewrite history. It is equivalent to the burning of inconvenient Jewish books by the Nazis in World War II.

The British have themselves had their rights to freedom of speech curtailed by both the courts and the pressure exercised by the now substantial Islamic lobby. This lobby demands 'respect'. It demands that no one may criticise the Prophet Muhammad or even portray a likeness of him. This demand affects Western democracy by curtailing the right to freedom of speech, the right to make comment regardless of giving offense.

The North - South divide.

Many have long suspected and this appears to have been confirmed in the expansion of the Eurozone that the industrious north of Europe would inevitably be subsidising the sunnier south. One only had to visit Greece for example to see what would previously have been called a Third World economy. It does appear in relation to the most crude analysis that wherever we find olives we find a lack of industrial organisation and activity. With the benefit of hindsight one could argue that Spain would qualify for this crude analysis; nonetheless who would have thought Spain would come to the brink of collapse?

Meanwhile back in the UK in May 2014 the housing market in London and the south-east is powering ahead with a growth rate of 10% per annum with the rest of the country lagging behind. The governor of the Bank of England Mark Carney has intervened to suggest that the buy to let government backed scheme is distorting the market and is a serious problem. There is much wringing of hands and almost universally a consensus within the media that the problem is that not enough houses are being built. Not a single commentator has referred to the demand side of the equation, i.e. that there are too many people chasing too few homes. How is this surging demand for homes being fuelled?

Well it must be immigration because we all know the indigenous population birth rate is relatively static. The country therefore faces the prospect of building on its cherished green belt land to accommodate a surplus of immigrants. In August 2014 we note there is a further intention by government to 'enhance' the terrorism laws which were introduced to deal with the by and large self inflicted problems of the second millennium. Self inflicted yes, by the irrational importation of millions of foreigners.

The Work Ethic.

Is it too crass to suggest that colder climates encourage harder work. Is it really too simplistic to suggest that the Protestant work ethic is itself a symptom of racial differences? Are races from warmer climates inherently and necessarily less industrious?

On 18 June 2014 sky News reported that the education select committee has found that white working class pupils perform worse than any other ethnic group with only 32% achieving five GCSEs or more at grade C level. The Chinese ethnic group scoring 77%, the Afro-Caribbean group scoring 62% and the Asian Indian group scoring 62%. This news and it isn't new news, is a startling and damning indictment of both our culture and our traditional work ethic. These figures are it appears a further nail in the coffin of the allegedly lazy English. The coffins and nails are invariably being imported. Seasonal workers, who are mainly foreign, in the agricultural industry are often cited as examples of English laziness.

These education performance figures need to be interpreted in the light of the other ethnic groups having English as a second language in the main part. Are the English so lazy and ignorant that they are unemployable and if so why? Are the English so demotivated, so disenfranchised and if so by whom, government policies, themselves, resentment? The message is clear! The English are destined if they are not already to become an underclass in their own country.

It is a relevant question to ask whether politicians are sidelining the English and actively encouraging mass immigration in order to boost the economy with people who are prepared to work harder for a lower wage? Is the economy paramount? It is legitimate to ask whether the English are entitled to remain in control of their country or whether the aspirations of politicians to improve the economy are of greater importance than a homogenous native population and the potential for civil unrest, the like of which we see in many other countries where ethnic tensions spill over occasionally into civil war e.g., Iraq; is a price worth paying for an ever growing economy? Per capita the economy appears in decline at the time of writing.

Spain. Greece. The democratic deficit. The single currency.

In March 2013 we note that the Italian population has voted for a hung parliament where no party has a majority and there were existing serious financial difficulties within the country. One of the candidates a former comedian had 25% of the popular vote. Italy is of course one of the larger economies in Europe and its national debt exceeds that of

Britain proportionately. Should the markets take fright and withdraw support from Italy, in which case then we can only guess at the outcome for the Eurozone and the Western economy at large.

In March 2013, following the public disorder in Greece and Spain we observed that Cyprus had sought a €10 billion bailout from the EU and as a consequence had unilaterally decided to levy a 10% charge on some bank accounts held in Cyprus to contribute to the country's economy. This was unprecedented in Western democracies and was arguably unlawful from the outset. ATM's in Cyprus were all sealed and Cypriots, visitors and service personnel alike were unable to withdraw funds from these machines.

Chapter 5

Compliance

The United Kingdom government places a great deal of reliability and confidence in the idea of trust and detailed regulations which they oblige the population to comply. The idea of trust has become a quaint British idea in modern times particularly so when with large numbers of diverse interests and peoples in the country it is evident that many do not share the ideal in these modern times.

It does appear anecdotally that the greater number of rules then the greater number of people there are who wish to try and break or bend them. We see the government complaining that larger companies use the governments own tax laws to avoid paying tax through the use of offshore tax havens and internationally agreed tax rules for companies trading across intra-national boundaries. Naming and shaming people and companies such as certain comedians and coffee shop chains exposes how fragile the substance of the country, government and compliance with the spirit rather than the law really is.

The so-called tax loopholes are not really loopholes at all they are perfectly reasonable bone fide means by which persons and companies can legally mitigate their tax liability. It is clear that the legislators are not smart enough to anticipate some fairly obvious so called loop holes. Lord Denning (together with many other Judges) on a notable historical occasion actually suggested that it was a right if not a duty that persons should be entitled to mitigate their taxes. This view and arguably an important democratic principle has been overturned by the recent general anti avoidance rules.

During the course of the author's daily life encounters occur with a number of people who are being 'cracked down' upon as the state through its various tax collecting agencies lets loose its angst on those prepared to bend the rules. They coerce, cajole and bully taxpayers into 'compliance'. The General Anti Avoidance Rules of 2013 saw in a desperate if not draconian attempt to regain control by the state.

On 10/12/13 we heard that 15 British soldiers had been found guilty of refusing to obey orders at a Court's Martial. The soldiers it appears were on a training exercise in Kenya: probably a bit of a jolly; when on parade they were ordered to stand to attention. They refused and sat down. The reasons for this insubordination they state was that they were led by 'muppets'. To those with longer memories this appears to have echoes of the First World War, 'lions led by donkeys'? We should not be too surprised at this insubordination when men can be lead out to the Brecon Beacons to die from exhaustion or exposure as a result of a lack of appreciation of the situation and planning. Nonetheless whilst the author would encourage a healthy disrespect for authority the appropriateness of this kind of behaviour in the armed forces is worrying. Even the Roman army however, or parts of it went on strike or worse from time to time for more pay or to get a new Caesar installed in place.

On the 25/11/13 we hear that the Royal Bank of Scotland (RBS) has been engaging in the practice of killing off businesses in order to acquire their residual assets at a knockdown price thus making substantial profits at the expense of their customers. On 4/12/13 we saw that there are further fines for rate fixing by RBS as part of a cartel, the fines totalling some £1bn to date. We also note the IT problems being encountered by RBS are actually having a negative impact upon customers who are having resulting difficulties at cash points.

In July 2014 we note that RBS has returned a profit of approximately £2.5bn and whilst the population at large pays its taxes through the 'PAYE' system many large organisations such as Starbucks, Google etc avoid paying taxes by perfectly legal means.

These failures to comply are symptomatic in a divided country. Put simply a 'them and us' culture. A culture which rewards incompetence and penalises hard work? The willingness to engage in criminal activity increases as do the number of TV expose's which demonstrate the ready market for fake passports and various other documents in the 'student' training and Visa industry.

Chapter 6

Politics and politicians

Arguably socialism is a force for evil. It serves no useful purpose other than to level down, redistribute taxes and to appeal to the scroungers in society. Socialism draws to itself those who lack enterprise, those who feel that others owe them a living. We see in May 2014 the debacle of the co-operative movement with the Co-op Bank technically insolvent and the Co-op group deficit at £2.5bn. Lord Myners' report suggested radical change, from a 21 strong volunteer board to a smaller plc type board with a number of key executives. Whilst the aims of the Co-op may be laudable we cannot escape the conclusion that socialism in all its forms is a bankrupt idea. It encourages laziness, a lack of accountability and those who think others should provide a living for them. On the other hand pragmatically socialism is of course a very attractive idea for those that have nothing to lose but may gain from it via the curse of redistribution of wealth.

Well what is society? We saw in the 1980s that Mrs Thatcher the then Prime Minister denied the existence of society. It is indeed true to say that the beginning of the decline of a cohesive homogenous society had begun years before her reign but there is little doubt that Mrs Thatcher contributed to the acceleration of the disintegration of the indigenous society.

Mrs Thatcher, born to humble origins in Grantham Lincolnshire in 1925 achieved success through determination and single-minded focus based on her humble roots. She succeeded academically in chemistry and became a barrister at law before becoming an MP. She was probably the greatest peacetime Prime Minister this country has ever known if measured in terms of the social changes made in so short a time.

In 1984 we saw the government take on the National Union of Miners using the police force to charge the ranks of miners protesting job losses, pay and conditions. Very few had sympathy with the miners leader Arthur Scargill who was seen by many to be a communist agitator; like the so-called 'Red Robbo' of the once great British motor industry years before.

Mrs Thatcher was a great protagonist for the Channel Tunnel and it was duly opened providing a wonderful opportunity for the French and illegal immigrants alike to continue the invasion of these islands. Baroness Thatcher died of a stroke on 8 April 2013. She was hailed as one of the greatest leaders and politician of modern times but reviled by all on the left of politics. She understood the evil of socialism, how corrupting and corrosive the welfare state can be. She understood that socialism undermined the work ethic and could become a lifestyle chosen for its ease, a far better option for many than work.

Despite her achievements based on simple work ethic ideas her memory is somewhat tainted by the strong possibility that she was aware of one of her closest aides preference for young children Sir Peter Morrison who was linked to the North Wales sex scandal.

We saw that Prime Minister Cameron proposed the 'Big Society'. He never quite explained what this was; it appears he may have had in mind a society where the spirit of the first and second World War was restored. A spirit where neighbour would help neighbour without seeking any sort of payback or remuneration. If that was the case then he was clearly 65 years and more out of date. He stated at one stage that society was broken. He presumably intended by way of this point to disagree with Mrs Thatcher's earlier observation that there was no such thing as society? Does he not realise that society has been broken by politicians and their policies and part of the reason for the demise of the indigenous 'society' is the lack of social cohesion and homogeneity caused by successive governments? Does he not realise that the British population by and large was the most accommodating, willing, patriotic and hard working possible?

Politicians come and go. They jolly and parade on the world stage and serve little useful purpose except for their own career's sake. They appear to not understand the forces at work in 'society' today, they do not appear to understand macro economics and it is evident that they have no idea let alone understanding of how to make things better. It appears they have been totally reliant on the utopian idea that macro economics will always feature economic growth. This is clearly and evidently a fallacy not only today but historically.

In early 2013 Chris Huhne was tried for the offence of perverting the course of justice. At the last moment he pleaded guilty at his trial and was subsequently sentenced. The trial arose because 10 years earlier he had conspired to offload some speeding penalty points on to his then wife Vicky Pryce. In more recent times he became divorced from his wife who decided she would have her pound of flesh and exposed the points conspiracy to the public. His ex-wife Pryce also being tried for conspiracy to pervert the course of justice. How the mighty are fallen! They both went to jail for a short time. Pryce since featuring on television interviews as an economics guru but with little to contribute.

Some weeks later we see the former chief executive of the Liberal Democrats party Lord Rennard being accused of sexual impropriety with office colleagues. In addition we saw the resignation of Cardinal O'Brien again in a flurry of press speculation as to inappropriate behaviour. What are these powerful people doing? Power corrupts, absolute power corrupts absolutely! After 10 years of chaos in Iraq and tens of thousands of deaths of innocent civilians we see Tony Blair, former British Prime Minister; not satisfied with his notable record of disasters to date advocating greater intervention by Britain in the then Syrian crisis in which it is estimated that 70,000 civilians had already perished by 2014.

In 2012 the home secretary decided to stem the flow of students from the Indian subcontinent. It had become quite evidently necessary because of the 'over- stays' and so-called students not actually studying but seeking employment. Early figures suggest that the restriction of student visas was actually reducing numbers seeking to come to Britain. In early 2013 however the Prime Minister David Cameron went on a visit to India, engaged in a cricket match with some young Indians he was promptly bowled out for a duck, as seen on TV. To add to this embarrassing spectacle of the naive Briton abroad Cameron then declared that any number of Indian students could come to Britain. This grovelling, cringing Prime Minister so desperate for trade embarrassed all.

It would be naive to suggest that politicians are going to be straight with people, otherwise how could they get into power in the first place in order to carry out their manifestoes. They promise the earth and deliver little but problems? The difficulty is however that the Prime Minister of the day given a majority has absolute power to do what he/she wants. This is not to deny the difficulty of coalition government which involves leading politicians who seem determined to be on the left or in the middle ground for their own sakes. Again perfectly understandable for those of us who recall our 'O' level statistics and the bell or normal distribution curve which states that the majority of the population's views will lie around the average, in political speak the middle ground.

We have seen an unelected Prime Minister Gordon Brown, a Scot reputed for his canny economic and 'prudent' financial management. In a very short space of time we saw however that despite this self-created reputation his management of the British economy, notwithstanding his predecessor Blair and the failings of the banking system turned out to be a disaster.

The difficulty appears to be the lack of experience and proper qualifications of politicians. George Osborne is a historian not an economist or accountant. He only recently came into politics and it is inconceivable that his record demonstrates the skill and necessary experience to manage a world size economy in such difficult circumstances, yet democracy 'obliges' the people to elect from a limited canvas those people who put themselves forward. Despite Osborne's apparent short-term success in the British economy as at July 2014 the underlying economy is weak, manufacturing is declining still and GDP per capita is down despite the celebrations. The only significant factors that are up are immigration and that the national and personal debt record levels were at £1.5 trillion.

David Cameron's Big Society idea was followed by his proclamation that society was broken. Well, who broke it?

Politicians! There can be no doubt about this it is they who pursue their often daft zealous ideas unfettered between elections, it is they who decide at vast expense to the UK public to meddle on the world's stage, it is they who decide that the country should punch above its weight in the ongoing pretence that Britain is still a major world power. It is politicians who insist on being on TV at all times instead of quietly getting on with the job and thinking strategically about the country's future. It is politicians who spend, spend, spend when the country is broke.

Would it be unreasonable to suggest that politicians should stop and think a bit more before pronouncing and making announcements which then result in an embarrassing U-turn or ideas that are quietly and conveniently forgotten when it becomes apparent that they are quite daft?

In April 2013 Baroness Thatcher died at the age of 87. She had been an MP for some 30 years and Prime Minister for 11 years. She is said to be one of the most divisive Prime Minister's ever to rule in the UK. She was undoubtedly decisive and held that market forces were pre-eminent and together with her erstwhile political ally Ronald Reagan waged war on communism during the Cold War period of the 20th century subsequently seeing the collapse of the Russian satellite states including East Germany.

It is difficult to capture the strength of feeling, then and personal attacks made against this significant politician of our time. The resurrection of the song from Judy Garland's Wizard of Oz 'Ding Dong the Witch is Dead' and the intention of many to celebrate her death perhaps says it all? Her funeral took place on Wednesday, 17 April 2013. It is evident from the strength of feeling and protests many of which are related to the 2013 timorous cuts in welfare expenditure e.g., the cap on benefits of £500 per week in relation to private rented accommodation, the tougher regime in relation to incapacity benefit, unemployment benefit etc, that communism is actually alive and well in the UK.

As benefit caps came into force in April 2013 we saw demonstrations, minority activism, public outrage and much wringing of hands from charities and the like. The population continually presented by the press and TV in particular with some poor single parent from some ethnic group or another with four, six or more children to support. They are being used to support the idea that such welfare cuts are inappropriate, unjust and terrible. What is of course really terrible is that the country should be in such a state so as to be able to attract such dependants who are unlikely ever to be able to support themselves and are supported at huge cost to the taxpayer. The taxpayer in question of course being unlikely very often to earn such sums as were being spent in benefits on these various groups.

We saw continuous political attacks by Messrs Balls and Miliband who want more jobs. As benefit caps came into force they argued that the government must create jobs. This would of course mean borrowing more because the only jobs that it is capable for government to create are government jobs. The size of the state remains enormous. Do they not realise this is partly how the UK got into a mess in the first place?

Who can doubt that most politicians are ignorant and are not qualified to carry out the serious duties that their various roles demand from them? They continually appeal to the public's most absurd instincts in relation to taxing A to benefit B, previously called re-distribution; now called progressive taxation by the cunning wordsmiths. This doctrine of redistribution can only go so far and can only be successful in relation to providing the most basic of support for those for example unable to work. Welfare surely cannot and should not provide a chosen lifestyle for those who will not work and wish to abuse the system?

On 18/11/13 we noted that Dennis McShane, former British Europe minister and MP; pleads guilty to false accounting and is awaiting sentencing. He numbers amongst the many MPs caught fiddling their expenses the most serious having been sent to jail previously. Britain's leaders!

Who said that the militant trade unions were dead? On 11/12/13 the trade unions have succeeded in securing a £350 'bonus' in order to avert a Boxing Day strike by tube drivers. Who can blame them when they see the continuing antics of politicians with Lord Bhatia OBE being exposed on the 4/12/13 following his appointment as chairman of EMF extracting in excess of £600,000 from the EMF (ethnic minority foundation) charity having previously been caught fiddling his parliamentary expenses.

In the third week of May 2014 we see the voluble Nigel Farage, leader of UKIP; register great success in the local council and European elections. UKIP leading the field in both with the Liberal Democrats being almost annihilated. Large questions surround the Deputy Prime Minister Nick Clegg and his future but no doubt he will continue in his customary pompous and patronising manner until being brought down completely by the people at the ballot box; his demise as MP of Sheffield Hallam being forecast on the May 2014 voting patterns.

On 4 June 2014 a number of media refer to the scandalous ongoing costs of PFI (Private Finance Initiative) contracts to the public purse. These contracts were placed by the last

Labour government and they were particularly supported by former Prime Minister Tony Blair who supported these financial devices. The front of the Independent is particularly effusive. These private finance initiative contracts were nothing more than expensive live now - pay later schemes. In contrast the politicians castigate the exorbitant interest rates charged by payday lenders who many argue provide a useful service to borrowers who cannot obtain credit from the usual institutions, i.e. the banks.

The end of the second week in June 2014 saw Prime Minister Cameron extolling the virtues of 'Britishness' and of course the subsequent attempts by commentators all and sundry to define the phrase. Let us not forget that Cameron is the man who also coined the phrase 'the Big Society' which seems largely to have been forgotten because few ever understood what it meant. Better efforts have however been made to define Britishness resulting in various sound bites including fairness, obeying the law, generosity etc. Cameron is attempting to get ethnic minorities to sign onto British values. Not at all unreasonable if it were not farcical. He just doesn't get it does he. People take their own ethnic identity wherever they go, they do not dump it, why because it is a fundamental part of them. Casting off one's identity would be rather like cutting off one's own nose to spite one's face.

In a generous and liberal society politicians are free to exercise whatever behaviour they choose. On 15 June 2014 we see a discussion between two eminent historians as to what Britishness means and in particular Cameron's reference to the Magna Carta of 1215. The historians could neither agree on the relevance or definition of Britishness or indeed whether the Magna Carta had anything whatever to do with the idea of Britishness.

Perhaps William Hague the Foreign Secretary was attempting to give us a clue as to what Britishness was when he told Sky news on 16 June 2014 that he estimated that some 400 UK linked or British citizens may be fighting with ISIS insurgents in Iraq and Syria. This is the reality. This is what Britishness means to some ethnic minorities many of whom think the British must pay for historical foreign adventures and mistakes. Having a British passport in one's possession does not mean one is British! If an Englishman is born in China does that make him Chinese, of course not.

In July 2014 we saw a Cabinet reshuffle with Prime Minister Cameron wielding the axe. William Hague resigned or was sacked as Foreign Secretary. The most striking change being the number of women appointed to the Cabinet, evidently another political move in order to attract women voters to cast their votes in favour of the Conservative party at the next general election in 2015.

We see Jean-Claude Juncker appointed as the head of the EU commission despite Mr Cameron's protestations. One of Mr Juncker's first pronouncements is that no further states will be admitted to the EU for five years. This appears to be a blow to the aspirations of a possible independent Scotland.

We see that on 4 August 2014, apparently a complete surprise to the Prime Minister David Cameron, that one of his ministers Baroness Sayeeda Warsi has resigned in protest at the government's apparent lack of action in relation to the Israeli/Gaza war. The 'Baroness', the first Muslim woman to be appointed to a British Cabinet shows her true colours in relation to where her loyalties lie. Britishness?

4th August 2014 a piece in City A.M features the Mayor of London Boris Johnson. The Mayor together with a number of economists are said to be highlighting the benefits of immigration to the City. The National Institute of Economic and Social research is said to hold the view that if the number of immigrants coming to the UK is reduced this will do long-term damage to the economy. A spokesman for the mayor said that controlled immigration has been and will continue to be good for London. On what basis he comes to these conclusions we do not know nor do we know on what basis he proposed an airport in the middle of the Thames estuary dubbed as Boris Island. A number of commentators are of the opinion that Boris' only interest is himself. A surprise?

A more widely held view amongst centre-right groups is that whilst immigration may have a positive effect on the economy in the short term and this is by no means proven; it is evident that public services are already feeling the strain from the existing huge influx of immigrants many of whom come to the country with some innately less healthy prospects than the indigenous population.

In the same fairly well respected newspaper we noted that Jim Wallace writes an article referring to businesses backing the mayor's call for EU renegotiation. It is quite striking, is it not that those politicians who have such an impact, often adverse; on our lives should be so disingenuous or downright ignorant about the nature of the EU treaties which with so many more members become virtually impossible to re-negotiate since any sort of renegotiation is simply not in the interest of the majority of the members of the EU who receive payments unlike the UK as a net contributor. Rabbits and lettuce?

On 11 August 2014 we see Dennis McShane, former Labour MP and minister for Europe being interviewed following his short prison sentence for fiddling his expenses. He invented receipts and payments and claimed for reimbursement accordingly. He made some interesting observations about his time inside, albeit for six weeks only out of the six-month sentence handed down. This coincided with a Channel 4 news item on the same day relating to overcrowding and the amount of contraband been smuggled into jails. The contraband includes drugs, mobile phones and the like. The news items related to the reduction of budgets and subsequent reduction in staff members with the rise to 29 prisons being in the 'serious concern' category. There is broad agreement now that the prison system is dysfunctional, is overcrowded and by comparison with other European countries it appears that judges appear to have a propensity in the UK to send people to jail for relatively minor offences. There is apparently little or no training being carried out in prisons where it is alleged that many of the prison officers are themselves corrupt and a part of the problem.

On 7 August BBC2 Newsnight reports on David Cameron's big Society. Jacob Rees-Mogg and others debate the topic. The idea of the big society was never properly defined by Cameron who to the cynical observer may appear to have attempted to hijack the credit in relation to all the good unpaid work carried out by thousands of volunteers, carers and the like. Rees-Mogg defended the idea but added little clarity to its definition.

Mr Blair, former British Prime Minister; together with Mr George W Bush the then American President took Britain into war in Iraq in 2003. We are all too aware of the consequences of that invasion in relation to the lives lost the cost of the adventure and the terrible loss of life and suffering. Mr Blair was rewarded with the highly paid post of envoy to the Middle East. We note that he was instrumental in introducing the private finance initiative and was largely responsible, notwithstanding the financial world wide crash for bringing the British economy further into debt and setting the scene for the subsequent vote for Scotland's independence.

The Scottish vote of 2 ½ million people was determining the future of the whole of the United Kingdom which comprises a further 62 million people who have no say in the matter despite the large financial contributions made to the Scottish economy in recent years. Minority rule? More taxpayers money is spent per capita in Scotland than in England and the Barnett formula is set to remain.

On 28 August 2014 we saw senior politicians including the Home Secretary Theresa May baying for the blood of the police and crime Commissioner for South Yorkshire. Politicians know full well that these posts are elected and independent of MPs. It was evident that this was a cynical ploy by MPs to be seen to be doing something when the total failure of Rotherham to protect younger vulnerable people is all too evident and responsibility does not lie at the door of one person, nor is it the system's fault. The fault lies with many senior highly paid people in both the police and the local authority who prefer the status quo than to doing their duty.

Calls for the blood of an individual by MPs and in particular the Home Secretary are perceived to disguise the fact that they have totally failed to protect the population from uncontrolled mass immigration from which a disproportionate number of offenders emanate. The office for National statistics reveals that net immigration to the UK was 243,000 people in the 12 months ending 31 March 2014 compared with the previous year when the figure was 175,000 people. These increases in the population of the UK are clearly unsustainable in relation to public services, infrastructure and surely the tolerance of the indigenous people. These figures are further evidence of the totally ineffective, incompetent senior politicians supposedly running the country. These same politicians had vowed to reduce the numbers coming to this country to the tens of thousands by 2015. Pigs might fly!

Chapter 7

The Cult of the Victim

What am I going to do if you do that to me? Where will I live if I am made homeless? How can I get along on £X per week benefits? Are these questions familiar? The cries ring out from the injured masses receiving assistance when they perceive assistance is insufficient, restricted, limited or cut off!

It appears that the welfare state has encouraged a lack of independence. Many would argue that single-parent families are being encouraged and, to an extent, some are a product of the state, that mass immigration is being encouraged but for what reasons? The answer is simple 'political populism', incompetence and apathy by those who pick up the bill. Such is the size of the entitlement culture that it is doubtful that a minority government can deal effectively in a single parliament with such huge problems.

The populist appeal of Miliband and Balls who lie on the left of politics and tell people that everything will be fine if they give them their votes is nothing it appears short of deceit. It is reasonable to propose that the pro-mass immigration lobby is unlikely to vote Conservative in future and therefore that socialism continues to be a popular chosen lifestyle for many.

Politicians must somehow attract positive people not negatives. Would it be unreasonable to suggest that the United States attracts strivers whilst the UK attracts skivers?

The US benefits system appears much less generous than the UK system.

The author has experience of the victim/benefits culture lifestyle and can assert that many of those who engage in this lifestyle do little for anyone else but themselves. As a chosen lifestyle the benefit recipient can bleed thousands of pounds from the taxpayer over many years. There are few reasonable checks incentives or a proper balance in the system. To receive benefits is merely a form filling exercise. Universal benefits are a magnet to many.

Khalid Aziz addressed this so eloquently on Channel 4 news on 15 April 2013. Khalid came to the UK from Pakistan, established a small business as a communications consultant and now employs a number of people. He held the view that it is not poverty that holds people back, it is poverty of aspiration. How true this is? Look at the plight of many white working class youths.

On 12/9/13 we saw a lady (allegedly) wearing a full face veil contesting the courts right to determine that witnesses should give evidence with their faces exposed. The judge ruling that she cannot give evidence unless the jury is able to see her face and its attendant expressions in order to come to their conclusions.

On 13/9/13 we noted that the Birmingham Metropolitan University withdrew its ban on hooded persons. It is now held that however that face veils, scarves and any other forms of dress that can vaguely be attributed to a cultural or religious practice <u>must be respected</u>.

On 6/11/13 the Secretary of State for defence became embroiled in a discussion in relation to the Portsmouth Naval shipyard which after 500 years of shipbuilding is no longer to build warships for the British navy. Hundreds of jobs are to be lost and many claim in the ensuing discussion that this decision is not economic but rather political insofar as shipbuilding jobs in Scotland appear to be protected. With a referendum available to the Scottish population only in October 2014 to determine the future of Scotland as either a part of the United Kingdom or an independent country; who could honestly say this major factor in the UK's future was not a consideration in awarding contracts?

On 21/11/13 a couple of Indian origin are arrested after three women were released from slavery in South London after 30 years. 30 years! The women are said to have been coerced and psychologically compelled to provide slavery services to the couple.

In November 2013 it was reported that 1485 cases of forced marriage were being investigated by the Metropolitan police since 2012. These cases are invariably amongst the 'Asian community' and very often include the coercion into marriage by so-called British Asians who have been persuaded to return to the subcontinent to discover their fate and identity of their spouse to be.

Most are acquainted with the practice of the Jewish community in relation to circumcision. No great fuss has been made about this over the years despite the fact that it is a form of genital mutilation. After all what politician wants to upset the 'Jewish community'? This matter will however will be revisited in due course since the number of Asian and Islamic women coming forward to speak out about FGM (female genital mutilation) is increasing by the day. What is quite alarming to the indigenous population; well that is to say those who give a damn; is that as at December 2013 there have been no arrests or prosecutions to date for these barbaric mediaeval practices, despite the sizeable cost of investigations!

The BBC Panorama programme on 23 June 2014 reported that 1.8 million households in the UK are waiting for social housing. Property prices in the London area continue to surge ahead reaching an annual increase of a staggering 20% in July 2014. Further discussion takes place as to the desperate need to build further houses in relation to the supply of housing. No reference is made whatever to the possibility of controlling the demand for housing i.e., the principal source being from immigration and subsequent birth rates.

Many assumed that Theresa May the Home Secretary, widely viewed as incompetent; would never succeed in the stated control target of tens of thousands of immigrants to the UK by 2015 (general election year) as opposed to the current hundreds of thousands.

The English as a culture are already blaming immigrants and foreigners for many of their ills. This resentment is almost certain to manifest itself in civil unrest in years to come: even the worm turns in due course! The inevitable consequence of this wait-and-see attitude is however self-destructive. The consequences of mass civil unrest and possible civil war in our cities and towns is unthinkable but becomes more likely by the hour.

On 4 August 2014 we note that a certain judge on a video link is heard to state that the victim's family in a parole hearing went to a great deal of effort to make what is known as their impact statement but that they did not realise that it was irrelevant. Inevitably for justice to be equitable this must be true, however there is a great deal of outcry and sympathy for Mr and Mrs McGinty, the victim's immediate family in relation to the judge's comments. We appear to live increasingly in a world of turbulent emotion rather than a world of rational behaviour.

It is evident that the 'nanny state' fosters the idea that many are victims and as such should be the recipients of the state's largesse. Someone must be responsible but it isn't me! In August 2014 we note that British politicians are considering legislation to prevent coercive or bullying behaviour in domestic intimate relationships. How the police and the CPS would deal with this is not clear but it is perfectly clear that this would be a tremendously difficult area to legislate for.

We have noted that some cultures within Britain oblige others to 'respect' them whether it is due or not for fear often of violence. These same cultures often treat woman as second class. This idea of respect is highly damaging to the idea of freedom of expression. From our personal experiences we are all too aware that the British state is both autocratic and benevolent, the difficulty is that these adjectives are often derived from the idea that autocracy is often manifest in the use of 'a sledgehammer to crack a walnut' and that benevolence is often offensive in its generosity to those who must pay for it.

It appears evident that the British Conservative Party is less conservative than 30 years ago in order to exercise any form of power. Note the power vacuum between 2010 – 15 with the coalition government. The counterweight to the conservatives being their partners the Liberal democrats lead by Clegg a left wing Euro fanatic. Like rabbits love lettuce 'progressive' socialism has great appeal to the 'have nots' who clamour for a 'fairer society'.

Chapter 8

The Police

It is said that in the UK the largely unarmed police force carries out its work with the consent of the general public.

The public may generally be unaware of some of the activities of the police including the compilation of a national public order database. This means the televising and collection of data of those who may march or protest in public. In a case in early 2013 Mr Catt a regular protester took his concerns before the court. The court held that the collection of data over an extended number of years by the police regarding this individual was unlawful and infringed his right to a private life under the Human Rights Act. This is an interesting matter given the fact that telecom's firms are obliged to retain data for 12 months and Islamic terrorism is increasingly a real concern in Britain.

The Conservatives in the coalition government of 2013 and in particular the Home Secretary Theresa May wished to exclude the UK from the Human Rights Act. The government was for years in the case of Abu Hamsa frustrated in their attempts to deport the individual. The frustration arose because the UK courts will not allow extradition to a country that may rely on evidence obtained by torture to mount a prosecution against Mr Hamsa. To deport Mr Hamsa would infringe human rights. Mr Hamsa was subsequently extradited to the United States and tried before a jury in New York, some 1 mile from ground zero.

Mr Hamsa being found guilty of terrorism offences was duly sentenced.

The Home Secretary argued in another case that by being unable to deport Abu Quatada that this may be an infringement of the rights of the rest of the population. This may well be so as this case has cost the taxpayer millions to date and there are numerous other cases of a similar nature. The question that some ask is whether the human rights act is of benefit to the majority of the population? This is often difficult to evaluate until one is directly affected by an infringement of our rights. The difficulty for most is to take the longer term view, the bigger picture as opposed to the immediate, expedient, political, short-term view. It may not be surprising to know that the coalition partners in government in 2013, the Liberal Democrats, were opposed to the abandonment of the Human Rights Act.

We see in May 2013 a frustrated Home Secretary Theresa May vowing yet again to deport this man at the request of Jordan but the courts resisting this on the grounds that his human rights may be infringed if tried by a court using evidence obtained by torture. Many in government would wish to see the Human Rights Act abolished and it has even been suggested the convention on human rights be suspended if not abolished in the UK. The reason for this is that it is become almost impossible to deport illegal immigrants if they have established a family and they assert their rights to a family life under the Human Rights Act 1998. Abu Quatada was eventually found not guilty in Jordan.

We saw examples of the Metropolitan police allegedly selling information for corrupt payments, persuading rape victims that they actually consented to sex, fitting up a government Minister (Andrew Mitchell), masquerading as 'climate camp protesters' and using false names during the course of developing relations with women protesters and having sex with them.

We hear much of home-grown terrorists. This invariably means men who have been born in Britain. We note in February 2013 three Birmingham born Muslim men were convicted of plotting major suicide terror attacks. These people are clearly the enemy within and have been inflicted on the population by successive politically correct governments. The government is aware that one in three terror plots occurs in the same areas and that government funding or more correctly taxpayers money is spent on a so-called anti-radicalisation programme. What this means is that money is spent in an attempt to persuade mainly young Muslim men they should not listen to those who wish to preach the doctrine of terror.

Muslim men appear over represented in the crimes of rape, sex trafficking, domestic slavery and general abuse. Huge amounts of taxpayer's money spent in trying to correct a self-inflicted problem imposed on the country by politicians therefore continues. We can however rest in the knowledge that this is democracy in action.

We note that the police had recorded 1700 rapes in the week before Easter 2013 including one reported rape taking place against a teenager on a bus as reported by Channel 4 News on 29 March 2013.

Such is the state of the country. The Dispatches programme on Channel 4 in March 2013 reported on the importation of puppies from Eastern Europe on forged pet passports. One of the difficulties around this illegal importation is the bypassing of the quarantine system and the importation of various diseases with the cuddly puppies which includes

Rabies and the Acino Cocus virus. This latter disease being capable of transfer to humans with deadly results.

No one can doubt the necessity for some form of police force and it would be naive to suggest that there would never be any corruption and wrongdoing in the police, we will all have our personal experiences no doubt? Equally it cannot be denied that the police like the rest of us are prone to temptation, a desire to protect their own backsides and stick together and occasionally to take inappropriate risks, bend the truth etc.

Probably the best case of known police malpractice is exemplified through their behaviour during and following the Hillsborough disaster of 1989 when 96 spectators died of crush injuries caused by the police in allowing too many people into a confined space and subsequently attempting to blame the spectators for their own demise. This classic case, which has yet some distance to travel in relation to proper conclusions; is recognised as being incompetence followed by a cover up by the police, judiciary and those in government. A national disgrace!

At demonstrations in London by students on 11/12/13 we saw the unholy spectacle of a police man punching a demonstrator in the face and knocking some to the ground. Later in the week we see police preventing a peaceful demonstration within the private grounds of a campus. Inevitably a degree of violence ensues from such confrontations where protesters see their inalienable right to protest being usurped by the police.

On 19/11/13 we see Metropolitan police officers appearing before the House of Commons select committee to give evidence on crime statistics and recording stating that in their view crimes are under recorded by the police by the use of a variety of devices which include 'discouraging reporting,' 'double counting' etc.

In June 2014 we see the Metropolitan police Commissioner again speaking to the topic of police corruption. He points out that the vast majority of police officers are honest and hard-working. We then see a contingent of the Metropolitan police in the early part of June 2014 digging up and examining waste ground, one of a number of proposed investigation sites, in Praia de Luz in Portugal. The police will be there for several weeks much to the annoyance apparently of the Portuguese authorities not to mention the local hoteliers and traders as the summer season gets underway. We may recall that the background to this case goes back seven years when the McCann family left a child's bedroom window open, went out to dinner leaving the children unattended to return later to find that their daughter Madeleine had been taken. Seven years on and at what must be an enormous cost would it be appropriate to presume that the McCanns are funding this ongoing extra ordinary effort and investigation out of the charity created for this purpose or is the British taxpayer paying for the British police still there interviewing suspects as 2014 drew to a close?

For two high status medically qualified parents to leave a child's window open whilst on holiday seven years ago must surely rank as gross negligence or contributory negligence? The McCanns returned to Portugal on 16 June 2014 to pursue the ex Portuguese police officer for damages in libel in the Portuguese court. The defendant had written a book stating that the McCanns had killed accidentally or otherwise their daughter and attempted to cover it up.

We saw on 14 July 2014 that the Commissioner of the Metropolitan Police Bernard Hogan-Howe announced a new recruitment policy stating that the Metropolitan police will only recruit from those who've lived in London for three out of the last six years. He states that this is in order for the police to be more representative. No one was observed to challenge the veracity or soundness of this sudden discriminatory policy announcement. Is it so desirable that the police reflect those they are to police? What we can be sure of is that this is positive discrimination in favour of minorities who are destined if not already to be a majority in the Greater London area. Is it unreasonable to observe at this point that the country's jails seem to have an overrepresentation of ethnic minority inmates? Does it follow and is it also unreasonable to observe that this may mark a further decline in the standards set for the capitol city's police force?

On 23 July 2014 the BBC News and other channels report on a further enquiry into police integrity in relation to a secret police operation of substantial proportions regarding victim's families. These victims include Stephen Lawrence's, Ricky Reel's family, Jean Charles de Menezes' family and others, a total of some 18 families/groups. All of these groups have it appears been spied on by the Metropolitan police knowing them to be innocent victims, in order it appears to obtain some compromising material on the families apparently to discredit them in relation to any claims they may have had or may pursue in future against the police. The public are assured that this covert police group is now wound up!

On 11 August 2014 we note that the Chief Constable of Greater Manchester Peter Fahey is being investigated for misconduct and that the Commissioner of the Metropolitan police has made its first arrest. Little being heard publicly since.

On 26 August 2014 we saw a senior police officer being interviewed by Channel 4 news in relation to the child abuse of 1400 in Rotherham. There is further commentary about this matter in the section on immigration which is notable in that the police together with the local authority are reported to have disregarded complaints of abuse which included physical abuse, sexual abuse which itself included the gang rape of girls as young as 11 years old by men of Pakistani origin. It appears the police and the local authority were more concerned about social cohesion than the criminal acts that were being committed.

On 28 August 2014 we note that a policeman in Yorkshire has been charged with an offence related to the inducement of an underage child to having sexual relations.

In August 2014 we see HMRC (Her Majesty's Revenue and Customs) have published their top ten rogues gallery. It is evident that the majority of the alleged miscreants are not from the indigenous population of Britain.

On 29 August 2014 we note the Metropolitan police publish pictures of 10 men they are seeking in connection with offences committed at the Notting Hill Carnival. They are all black. On the same day we see further discussion about the 'disgraceful' conduct of the police when carrying out 'stop and search' operations in London. Heaven forbid the police are accused of ethnic profiling! This practice must of course be stopped and clearly the most effective way is to adopt the Commissioner's policy of positive discrimination in recruitment.

On the 31 August 2014 we note that the Hampshire police have travelled to Spain and obtained a European arrest warrant for the parents of a child taken from a local hospital against doctors advice. The parents stated they were seeking treatment not available on the NHS. Noting the police trip to Portugal in the McCann's case earlier in 2014. Was this not, typically, a little heavy handed? This pretence that the state is in control of all matters shortly after the scandal of the Rotherham child abuse saga has been publicised emphasises the autocratic side of government.

We can all put their hands up and say that we are not perfect but the police are there to set an example in the way they conduct themselves because of the importance of their role and that they have the power of arrest over the people. People are entitled to expect that the police are paragons of virtue, unfortunately they are constantly proven to be less than virtuous and the public are disappointed.

Chapter 9

World population

The world's population has exceeded 7 billion, 1/6 of which are Chinese. Chinese families are limited to one child per family or otherwise they suffer the wrath of the state. A 'surplus' child was featured in the news on 28th of May 2013 being rescued from what appeared to be a 100 mm soil pipe downstream of a lavatory. Was this the influence of state regulation, a mother in mental turmoil, poverty or plain attempted murder?

Whilst China may have too many people Western attitudes are somewhat different and a great deal of taxpayers money is spent for example on IVF (invitro fertilisation) in the UK. One may argue this from a number of points of view. Clearly a couple desiring children will go to whatever lengths are necessary to acquire a family. These lengths include adoption, kidnapping of other people's children, IVF and so on. Given that the British are constantly bombarded with charitable appeals to provide or adopt the starving children of Asia or Africa perhaps we should be considering the redistribution of children rather than focusing substantial resources on IVF? Probably more to the point, if so many children born in what is now called the developing world are then subjected to starvation perhaps the world should be focusing its efforts on the prevention of children being born that cannot be adequately cared for. Contraception perhaps?

The growth in Chinese wealth seen in recent years is quite extraordinary. The one-party Communist state is obliged to control its people with an iron fist. Cash rich China has invested heavily outside its borders. The secret of its success is the low pay for the majority of its workforce which per head is amongst the lowest in the world. Britain can only dream of such growth in its economy but cannot possibly achieve it because of the dead weight of the state, the benefit system, the welfare state in general and the oppressive manner in which regulation is applied.

We continually see on British TV the plight of many children and adults who are unable to feed themselves in undeveloped countries. These undeveloped countries often have undemocratic leadership models and corruption is known to be rife in many of them. Some commentators have observed that certain natural population control mechanisms are being subverted by political correctness or misplaced kindness. Darwin's theory of evolution being replaced by socialism, the end game being that every one dies through overpopulation? The survival of the fittest or no-one?

As the population of the world expands and weather patterns and trouble spots erupt mainly from the manifestation of Islamic terrorist groups we see that great movements of population are inevitable and are already occurring in 2014 in Syria and Iraq. It is evident that a favoured destination for many displaced persons is the UK. Many aspire to be refugees because it is relatively easy to gain access to the UK and its generous support system.

We saw the French in Calais again being requested by the British to close down one of the immigration camps thrown up by refugees and economic migrants determined to reach the shores of the 'promised land', the UK. We noted that Nick Clegg had realised his open door policy on immigration to the UK was not good for the forthcoming election of 2015 and unsurprisingly changed his position.

In the middle of August we saw a shipping container at Tilbury being discovered, more by chance than judgement. It contained 35 occupants from the Indian subcontinent one of whom was found to be dead on arrival. As a result of pull factors we saw that disadvantaged people will face almost any risk and pay traffickers to get to the UK.

It is evident that much of the world's population cannot feed itself but continues to breed at a prolific rate. It is also evident that charities and modern drugs and their availability are fuelling increases in the world's population to the extent that Darwin's theory arguably no longer applies. This means that there are few challenges, caps or tests to control the size of the population which continues to surge. The teaming masses of West Africa can survive even Ebola with the help of the West.

Chapter 10

Regulation

Britain is a highly regulated country to the point of being oppressive and incomprehensible. There are so-called safety cameras on our highways, cameras in high streets, in banks and in transport systems. We see that the law is aggressively applied to the unwary members of the population for relative misdemeanours such as speeding and other matters whereas errors more serious caused directly by government are overlooked. Never has it been more true that government requires the population to do as it says not as it does. The governed are it appears a different species to those in power. A defining issue about power is of course the use to which it is put. It is evident from the turmoil and continuous state of chaos in the UK that the government is overwhelmed by events, incompetent and completely out of its depth.

There is evidence to suggest that political pressure has been exerted on the tax collectors in the UK. This leads to the possibility that it is 'leaning' on small companies who for example in their formative years may be fragile. This pressure can have the effect of distracting small company managers from making profits by virtue of the time and costs taken to deal with such matters. This puts small companies under even more pressure in an existing seriously challenging financial climate. Are we seeing the return of a form of McCarthyism? In a recent recruiting campaign the government's tax collectors stated that 'they were determined to reduce the deficit' and it appears they will bend rules to serve their political masters in this aim.

On Monday 1st August 2014 a number of newspapers report that the Finance Bill 2014 has received Royal assent. The bill now contains legislation which will enable HMRC (Her Majesty's Revenue and Customs) to presume that taxes may be owed rather than have to prove it is. This dangerous and authoritarian approach to tax collecting means that the taxpayer in certain circumstances has to pay a tax bill then attempt to prove that it was not due. This reverse burden of proof is not new in law indeed the Council Tax legislation provides similar rules. The criminal law also increasingly presumes that a person must prove his innocence in appropriate cases eg, terrorist offences, the production of insurance if involved in a driving or traffic matter, etc.

On the 27 August 2014 we note that politicians are calling for anyone travelling to Syria or Iraq to inform the authorities before they travel. Failure to inform the authorities could lead to a quasi admission of guilt in relation to unspecified terrorism offences. This desperate suggestion only underlines how inadequate governance is in Britain.

Regulation – what regulation? Hector Sants former boss of the FSA (Financial Services Authority) during the financial meltdown of the UK economy quietly slipped away from the limelight to become <u>Sir</u> Hector Sants and is now head of a non government organisation.

Meanwhile on 3 September 2014 we noted of equal importance to newscasters that the largest democracy in the world has a young Indian girl of 18 years old marrying a stray dog in order to remove a curse!

Chapter 11

Education

The education system in Great Britain has been tampered with substantially in the last 50 years. These constant changes represent a moving target to both the young people concerned and potential employers alike. The changing standards are themselves self defeating since only educationalists and specialists understand what a particular qualification means. It is evident from the remarks of employers that modern qualifications have it appears been 'dumbed down' to the extent that they are no longer accepted as benchmarks on which to base offers of employment. If it aint broke, don't fix it?

Over the years we have seen a reduction in employment opportunities in traditional craft skills and a huge emphasis on obtaining university degrees. The Blair government went so far as to initiate a target of 50% of the population in education at univerity. The Universities of course welcomed this since it meant swelling their ranks with substantial increases in funding with which to deploy in salaries, research etc. We saw the burgeoning of degrees in every conceivable subject adding further to the confusion of prospective employers.

In 2013 data was published suggesting that English students at age 16 were some two years in academic attainment behind their South Asian counterparts.

In addition to a UK report on 13/10/13 the OECD published a report it had carried out on 24 Western democracies. The report included the USA, which did not fare well; also many European countries and the UK. It was disappointing to see, but not surprising, that in England the rankings for both numeracy and literacy were fairly close to the bottom i.e. 22nd and 24th.

On 18 June 2014 Sky News reported that the education select committee found that white working class pupils perform worse than any other ethnic group in England with only 32% achieving five GCSEs or more at grade C level. The Chinese ethnic group scoring 77%, the Afro-Caribbean group scoring 62% and the Asian/Indian group scoring 62%. What is going wrong? Typically, it appears, that there is no simple single answer to this vexing problem.

It appears evident that if the country's standards as a whole are lacking relative to other countries and if the working class indigenous population in educational terms is close or at the bottom of the pile then there are little prospects for the English working classes to compete on the world stage and now of greater concern in their own country.

In August 2014 we saw the A-level results published with the numbers of many grades at higher level recorded as an increase on previous years, however that results are generally poorer.

Chapter 12

The Financial Crisis 2008

Traditionally society has, with the exception of a significant minority of scroungers related to the concept of 'a fair days work for a fair day's pay'. Whilst historically England has occasionally been identified as the sick man of Europe in relation to the antics of a significant proportion of the workforce, e.g. the now defunct British owned car manufacturing industry, railway workers and the like over the years: since the war steady financial progress was being made in the country. There were never great export surpluses but equally there was also not a £1.5 trillion national debt until recently.

Mr Blair, a recent Labour Prime Minister who served for 10 years before handing over power to Gordon Brown the so-called prudent chancellor introduced the concept of PFI the private finance initiative. Through PFI the socialist governments between 1997 and 2005 built many hospitals and schools but at what cost? The PFI principle relies on private finance to fund the building of national infrastructure but on terms which are prohibitively expensive in the long run. Live now let our children pay later? This is a great embarrassment to government since the exorbitant cost of PFI coupled with some major financial disasters in defence procurement, the development of computer systems for the NHS and other arms of government continues thus bringing the economy to its knees.

In 2014 given the huge burdens imposed on the taxpayer by the various PFI schemes introduced by government we see that payday lenders were being castigated by government albeit they provided a service to individuals.

Who would have thought that such a huge debt burden largely created by the previous Labour government would result in the Labour opposition in 2013 demanding further expenditure in order to stimulate the economy during what was as close as can be to a 'triple dip' recession. We saw Mr Balls shouting from the opposition front bench his recommendations for re-stimulating the economy himself having been one of the architects of the country's perilous financial state of affairs.

We saw that the British economy in the hands of Mr Cameron and Osborne appeared with such little imagination to ineffectively attempt to reduce the country's debt burden. Their tactics were clearly not working and in February 2013 the rating agency Moody's downgraded the British economy from AAA to AA1. We noted in passing that Mr Osborne has no qualifications in financial matters nor any previous experience in the macro affairs of any large entity himself being a 2:1 graduate in history.

One of the many serious side-effects of the financial crisis of 2007/8 was the insolvency of some of the U.K.'s major banks, RBS and Lloyds TSB being but two. At the end of February 2013 the 80% taxpayer owned bank RBS reported huge losses yet again in excess of £5 billion. We saw that some of our banks have been fined huge sums for fiddling the 'LIBOR' rate, for the mis-selling of personal protection insurance and for the mis-selling of interest rate swaps to small businesses whom some forced out of business and then asset stripped.

It is quite extraordinary that banker's bonuses were paid by the RBS bank in excess of £600 million in 2012. It was suggested that pay rates must be competitive otherwise highflying talented people will leave the banks. On the same day a proposal was made by the Eurozone to bind member states to a maximum bonus payment to any banker of not more than their annual basic salary. This quite extraordinary proposed intervention in the 'free market' was a yet further sign that the Eurozone is totally out of touch with the reality of markets and free trade and is in fact an undemocratic socialist political cartel.

On 28 February 2013 two employees of the U.K.'s serious fraud office were charged and appeared in court with conspiracy to commit fraud in the sum of £1 million. On the same day it was reported that the Ministry of Defence had been found to have made unnecessary procurement of equipment purchases exceeding £1.5 billion pounds. It is accepted that these procurement matters are complex and require a degree of crystal ball gazing but we are equally dealing with large numbers. This was not the first time that the MoD has come under fire in their epic and apparently timeless criminal incompetence.

Who can doubt that the UK and Europe at large is in meltdown? Social cohesion, the financial system and more importantly capitalism are being challenged as never before. The problem is not capitalism. All British governments in recent times have made unsustainable promises to the people to acquire their votes. The real question arising from this chaos, mainly caused by incompetent governments; was and is how to move forward from the mess.

In the early part of 2013 'fairness' was the great watchword for all politicians because of course no one can deny that society should be fair, but can it be? Fairness must by definition, taking the innate character of homo sapiens into account, be unattainable. Fairness is the beating heart of socialism as is the concept that all men are equal. Both propositions are arguably nonsensical. Even in communist China we see that fairness is the last concern of those in power. In Russia too but of course the Russians have realised the fallacy of communism and have abandoned it accordingly. Most people realise that the benefits of capitalism far outweigh the disadvantages of its alternatives which arguably lead to greater corruption.

There is a difficulty here with this argument of course, as we sink further into financial decline the underclass increases in size and consequently those with a predisposition to the idea of the redistribution of wealth are increasing in number. As numbers of the poor inevitably increase so does civil unrest as we witnessed in the London riots of 2012. The disenfranchised increase in number and so does the demand to redistribute the wealth of the 'haves' to the 'have nots'. As we have seen if government will not redistribute then the 'have nots' will take what they can. This does of course mean the breakdown of society and anarchy at large.

The government in 2013 decided its priority must be to reduce the national debt. This is long overdue and probably too late. A previous Labour government effectively ran the country into the ground and during its last throes in power Liam Byrne a government minister proclaimed "there is no money left". This was entirely correct but was an optimistic statement of the problem, what he meant was there is no borrowed money left. With a growing £1.3 trillion debt at the time the country could not possibly recover due to the growing dead weight of the welfare state. This is not a simple matter to resolve because as we have seen inevitably we shall have people out on the streets rioting and protesting as previously seen in Greece and Spain.

In April 2013 the report on the management of the RBS crisis was published and the three leading figures within the organisation were castigated in public to the extent that calls were made for them to be barred from acting as directors of companies in future. Consideration was given to prosecuting three senior managers with a view to recovering lost funds. One of the former RBS employees was compelled by public opinion to resign his current post on the board of directors of a different large company.

We note at the beginning of December 2013 the continuing saga of the banks with Lloyds bank being fined £28 million for pressuring its staff to sell unwanted products to its customers. The incentives were rather more stick and carrot it appears with staff being demoted or their pay reduced if they didn't meet targets. One employee is said to so desperately have wanted to make sales he sold the product to himself, his family and friends in order to meet his target.

Those persons with an interest in the finances of the country and particularly those who subscribe to such publications as the Money Week magazine will have noticed that even under the coalition government of 2013 the debt mountain continued to climb and was forecast to reach £1.3 trillion in the foreseeable future. £1.5tr in 2015. Money Week contributors forecast the potential collapse of the economy and social unrest as a result of this irresponsible borrowing by successive previous governments and the present incumbents. It is interesting to note that no government has succeeded in climbing out of a debt hole so deep and that the UK debt as a proportion of its GDP exceeds the debt levels of the Weimar Republic prior to the Second World War.

In June 2014 we saw house prices in south-east reaching another high and discussion between politicians and the Bank of England in relation to controlling the rate of growth of house prices so as not to cause a boom and bust bubble. There is continuing discussion about building more houses, the supply of which is clearly lacking. There is little or no discussion about the causes of the substantial rise in prices in the south-east of approximately 15+%. Those commentators who are prepared to address this demand part of the fundamental supply and demand equation; conclude that the demand is fuelled mainly by immigration.

In July 2014 we saw George Osborne Chancellor of the Exchequer commenting on recently released figures which suggest that UK GDP has reached the level it was during the crash of 2007/8. This was certainly good news but has severe limitations when considered against the relevant background. The background factors were that the UK population had grown by 5% in the same time and therefore the return of GDP to 2008 levels was some 6% less on a per capita basis and took no account of inflation. We saw that manufacturing output and agricultural output figures were down. The poor export figures and unsustainable debt burden were however referred to by certain minority commentators who forecast a substantial crash into the future.

Chapter 13

Freedom of Speech, the Press and the Leveson enquiry

Following an extensive public enquiry Lord Justice Leveson recommended a form of self-censorship by the press with statutory backing. The self-censorship being backed up by a so-called independent statutory body. It could not seriously be argued that this would not be the end of free speech in the press. Furthermore the coercive forces at work in this matter suggested that those newspapers that do not voluntarily sign up to the self censorship regime will be penalised for not doing so should they at any time in future be found to be errant. Cohersive?

A very vocal campaign calling itself 'hacked off' and claiming to speak on behalf of victims including the Dowlers, the McCanns, Hugh Grant and the like vigorously sought to end press freedom by supporting the Leveson recommendations. English men and women have fought and died to secure democracy and press freedom. Without press freedom there is no democracy. No matter what they say governments and people in power will by the nature of the human condition inevitably seek on occasions to abuse that power. Politicians have and will continue to seek to fiddle their expenses and abuse their positions in a multiplicity of ways in their own self interests.

Without press freedom politicians and the police would not be exposed for their own criminal activities and abuses of power. Ian Tomlinson who died as a result of a police assault in London was filmed by onlookers may have been unmentioned had it not been for modern technology and 24-hour news.

In March 2013 we see Prime Minister Cameron nonetheless stoutly defending freedom of the press despite the objections of his coalition partners and in particular the Deputy Prime Minister Nick Clegg who wished to see freedom of the press curtailed. The Labour Party headed by Ed Miliband joined in the chorus to curtail freedom of the press allegedly so that victims may have justice. What they fail to recognise or acknowledge is that dozens of arrests have been made in relation to phone hacking and the massive Metropolitan police investigations into press malpractice continued for years. The arrests have included police officers and others in public service. The law was therefore arguably more than sufficient to deal with any abuse by the press; but the country, its politicians, save a notable few; have descended into a mob seeking popularity and the scoring of cheap, populist, political points.

It cannot be right in this matter or any other, that the interests of the majority and democracy should be dictated to by the relatively few albeit innocent victims, no matter how grievously they have been wronged. We need politicians who are prepared and able to take a principled view rather than to count every single potential vote.

In May 2013 we saw the Prime Minister David Cameron rejecting the newspapers rejection of the proposed press regulation. Despite the apparent doublespeak this Prime Minister had no concept it appears of what freedom of the press meant or its importance to the British unwritten constitution nor the consequences for democracy and the people of this country if politicians were to have in any measure a say or control of the press. It is clear that many politicians would like to see the press regulated and under their thumbs for reasons that are all too obvious not least the recent exposure of the fiddling, theft of public money by politicians, duck houses and the like.

In October 2013 following agreement of the three main political parties on a form of regulatory system the New Statesman's Fraser Nelson stepped forward to declare he would not have his newspaper sign up to any press regulatory body or agreement where there was any involvement from government. Fraser Nelson a hero and his principles were not universally commended.

The Independent took an independent view and declared that it had no problem signing up for the agreement of the press to be regulated based on the model agreed by the three main political parties of the day. Is it not quite shocking that a country calling itself a democracy should even attempt to curtail the freedom of the press because a handful of people had been offended i.e. Hugh Grant, the McCanns, the Dowler's etc?

How 'surprising' it was to see barristers, a number of senior people in public life and the like leading a campaign the ultimate objective of which was to curtail the freedom of the press because some had been personally upset. It is important to consider that no doubt some people had been wronged and for the record many of them have received handsome payments in relation to the wrongs committed against them. The police interviewed and charged numerous persons from the media, or previously employed by the media; with a variety of offences related to phone hacking, misconduct in a public office etc.

On the 30th October 2013 the privy Council approved the form of press regulation agreed by the three main political parties. How dangerous is this for a democracy? That the politicians of the day should have any say or influence on whatsoever is printed or broadcast sounds the death knell of freedom of expression, a human right and democracy. The great desire of politicians is to have power at their fingertips without the challenges and investigative journalism which has exposed so much corruption in the political system. A written constitution urgently needed!

In November 2013 the offices of the Guardian newspaper were 'raided' by the secret service and the editor Alan Rusbridger was 'invited' to destroy certain computer components containing allegedly top-secret matter provided to it by a 'whistleblower'. He complied it appears.

Attacks continue on the freedom of expression both at the European level and national level. The European court of justice in the spring of 2014 declared that a Spanish applicant may insist that Google remove factually correct historical information about him. This astonishing ruling appears to conflict with the EU's own human rights Charter and was the most blatant and authoritarian attempt to rewrite history to date. If a person is being wrongly held to account for information which is incorrect then that is a different matter and should be corrected but to make an authoritative ruling as to the deletion of factually correct historical data from a website is beyond printable words for fear those words themselves be censored!

On 23 June 2014 three Al Jazeera journalists were sentenced to 7 years in prison for reporting the news in Egypt. Sue Turton a former Channel 4 news presenter was sentenced to 10 years in absentia. It is evident from the Leveson enquiry which attacked press freedom, the secrecy of government and their desire to curtail the press supposedly often on the grounds of privacy, the EU's desire to rewrite history and erase historically correct items from the Internet and much more; that freedom of speech and of the press is something that must continue to be fought for.

On 23 July 2014 we heard from various news broadcasts that a liberal Democrat MP in Bradford has made remarks to the effect that if he was in Gaza during the current escalation of the Middle East conflict, then he would probably have fired rockets at Israel as well. This was subsequently discussed on Newsnight with Baroness Jenny Tonge and a Conservative MP himself with Kurdish roots. With typically poor chairmanship the discussion descended into an argument about the merits of the Israelis and Arabs visiting warfare upon each other. During the course of the discussion they completely disregarded the point which is that freedom of expression is the right to express opinions whether or not others disagree with them.

The dangerous trend in views and beliefs against the freedom of the press is of great concern to the English. It is becoming evident that non-indigenous members of the community often demand 'respect' whether it is due or not. The effect of this is to stultify opinion. The author recalls on one occasion when visiting a high street shop a shop assistant decided that a potential customer when questioning him about a technical matter held that the customer was being disrespectful and refused to serve him.

Chapter 14

Employment, The Monarchy, Foreign Interests and Privatisation

The cradle of the Industrial Revolution England has seen many changes. In the mid-Victorian age employers exploited the workforce and exposed them to great dangers which resulted in workers organising themselves and subsequent legislation to protect the workforce. The trade unions were born and created the Labour Party. No one can argue that safety precautions at work should be disregarded but the continuing effects of legislation and socialist rights have eroded flexibility and the rights of employers to hire and fire.

We see that huge numbers of immigrants have come to the country, in East Anglia we saw vast numbers of so called seasonal workers from Eastern Europe in the arable fields. We have seen Asians arrive in droves. They have been prepared to work long hours for low pay. It was estimated in 2014 that 10% of the population was from immigrant stock and inexorably rising as a result of their more prolific birth rates. Is it a surprise that the indigenous population should feel already disenfranchised by the year 2014? Taken together with a resistance to education particularly amongst working class white people it was no surprise that the unemployed included a growing number of young white men. The government creates employment schemes designed principally to get people back to work. This is all very well if there were jobs for people to do of course!

We noted that earlier in February 2013 government statistics suggested that only 3.6% of those attending government work programmes actually realise jobs in employment. This dismal success rate arguably exposes the smoke and mirrors approach to real problems by government. In the meantime we had huge numbers of unemployed all drawing benefits which includes the hugely expensive housing benefit and its successor scheme.

The demography of employment appeared to suggest that the pattern of full-time working and guaranteed employment was a thing of the past. We observed an increase in part-time insecure types of work but also an increase in unemployment. Whilst the flexibility of the marketplace was welcome to many, except some diehard socialists and trade unionists; there was little doubt that these were symptoms of a developing world stagnant economy.

The BBC News on 19 June 2014 reported on Iain Duncan Smith's employment and support allowance failing to get people back into work and that the costs of this 'measure' were rocketing beyond its benefit.

In 2014 we saw that the pattern of employment was changing dramatically in other respects with the number of self-employed having grown considerably. There were many self-employed relatively low paid jobs and a substantial increase in the number of zero hours 'hire or fire' contracts. This poor economic performance was set against the inevitable prospect of a mortgage interest rate rise in the future.

The Monarchy.

Accident of Birth. Privileged classes. Sustaining the class system. The honours system. The House of Lords.

Bradley Wiggins, a recent winner of the Tour de France cycle race; was knighted by her Majesty the Queen for services to cycling. Yes that's right, 'services to cycling'. Bradley, Kilburn born and a modest man stated that he felt 'humbled'. Yes that's right, humbled at being elevated. Much touching of the forelock. That's it ma'am – keep them in their place. One can only bestow honours on another from a superior higher position.

On 4 June 2014 we saw the Queens speech held in Parliament, a rich pageant of pomp and history. There are 11 measures within the Queen's speech for the remainder of the Parliament all overshadowed on the day by a spat between Theresa May the Home Secretary and Michael Gove the Education Secretary about who was responsible for having done nothing to prevent Islamic extremism being discovered in the schools around the country and in particular in Birmingham.

In August 2014 we see Karen Brady being elevated to the peerage. She could now keep company with her east end chum Alan Sugar in the House of Lords. Lady Brady has a certain ring to it!

Very few people decline to be honoured, quite naturally. But if we take a look at the bigger picture it is fairly evident that these honours doled out by the monarch, including to the likes of Jimmy Savile and Cliff Richard are symptomatic of a society still structured around class and privilege. The honours system props up the outdated status quo and of course provides a great deal of satisfaction to the Royal family in that they receive much humble gratitude from their obsequious 'subjects' on whom honours are bestowed.

Foreign interests.

The UK is seen to be an open door for all! We see mass immigration from East European countries, from Russia, Africa, China, Asia and Southeast Asia. Among this flood there have been some notable Russian so-called oligarchs basing themselves in the London area investing in football clubs and the great passion the British have for this game.

We saw a number of unexplained deaths within the Russian immigrant community and notably those who may have involved themselves in disputes with the Russian government in one way or another. All this takes place whilst the English look on in passive bemusement. Or are they amused?

In December 2013 we see the Tory government proposing to charge foreign owned properties with capital gains tax in order to secure income and allegedly to damp down the demand for the purchase of investment properties particularly in the London area, many of which are never occupied. Until 2013 very few people were aware that foreign held properties were not charged to capital gains tax.

Privatisation of gas, water, electricity utilities. The privatised railway system. Subsidised public transport.

The UK has seen some extraordinary developments in relation to the selling off of its utilities to foreign companies. Who would have thought 20 years ago that many of the electricity and water supply companies would be in foreign hands? Who would have thought, with the exception of British Road Services, that we would see the wholesale privatisation of the railways. There are two major problems with the sell-off's, firstly the lack of control that the sell-off brings in relation to what must surely be a fundamental part of the country's infrastructure and secondly, the subsidising of certain privatised entities which appears to be an ongoing matter by the taxpayer, eg rail. One might have thought that these subsidies would have brought about a decrease in fares? No, these events have served only to enhance the profits of the entities concerned from the sale of these cash cows providing arguably ever decreasing standards and price rises well above inflation.

In November and December 2013 we saw the politicians turning somersaults in relation to the opposition leader's comment as to the increasing cost of living for ordinary people. These comments are made against a background of substantial rises in energy costs triggered by what appears to be 'co-operation' between the big six suppliers. Such co-operation being unlawful in EU law.

We saw in the UK in 2014 that a large number of utilities are controlled by foreign interests. These business cash cows are often the subject of much controversy in that the charges they make are seen by many to be exploitative. The water companies are in a more enviable position than others in that they are not subject to competition at all and are true monopolies. Whether it is right and proper for utility companies and the basic transport systems to be in private ownership is a huge question in itself. It is of course as much a political question as a commercial one and those on the so-called right wing of politics might conclude that all of these systems should be in private ownership providing there is adequate competition and other necessary and appropriate safeguards. By this means they might argue that trade unions are unlikely to become dominant and hold the public to ransom, eg, tube strikes etc. Perhaps there is a balance to be sought in relation to essential services and infrastructure?

Chapter 15

Mass immigration

It appears that British politicians since the 1950's decided that mass immigration to Britain was a good thing? The so-called right-wing parties BNP etc have continuously argued that mass immigration was never put to the British people and is therefore an undemocratic act. It appears to many that mass immigration has brought few benefits and many problems. We can note with reasonable certainty that unemployment within ethnic communities is higher than the indigenous population and this is sometimes stated to be as a result of prejudice or the innate 'racism' of the indigenous population. We can also observe that particular medical issues are brought into the country with immigration including sickle-cell anaemia. It also appears that a high degree of gun crime and gang warfare results from certain ethnic minority communities.

In early March 2013 we were advised by the British 'Diabetes UK' that 4.6% of the UK population now has type I and 2 diabetes. The source of this upsurge is apparently related to the weight and age and ethnic groups. At the time these figures were released we note that the NHS and overseas aid are the only protected areas within government budgets where every other public sector is being slashed. Do UK politicians feel some obligation to secure the interests of foreigners at the expense of their own people? Enoch Powell stated he had never seen a country so enthusiastically heap fuel on to its own funeral pyre?

The population is constantly reminded that black athletes bring great honours to this country and there is little doubt that Mo Farah is a great athlete. He drapes the British flag around his shoulders and celebrates his Britishness. Is he British? He has a British passport. The answer to the question must be certainly yes! So we can say that anyone holding a British passport is British. What we cannot say is that immigrants holding British passports are English, Welsh or Scottish. If an Englishman goes to China and obtains a Chinese passport or to Japan and obtains a Japanese passport, very unlikely! Then he is certainly not Chinese or Japanese.

We can see all around us the effects of redistribution and socialism. Housing benefit for example. Combined with council tax benefit and the obligation of local authorities to provide housing to homeless persons, save those who have deemed to have made themselves homeless; this provision provides an open goal in society at huge cost to the hard-pressed taxpayer. It is increasingly intriguing to many that the indigenous taxpayer has been so docile and laid-back about these impositions not to mention the increasing aggressive tendencies we see in society from many immigrants.

It is important to emphasise that prejudice is by definition to prejudge, we do not need to prejudge we now have more evidence than enough to demonstrate that certain ethnic minorities are more disposed to crime, the use of guns, the abuse of women including the barbaric practice of FGM, to commit terrorist attacks and to generally have a disrespect both for the culture and traditions established over thousands of years in Britain.

During March 2013 numerous unemployed were paraded on television to emphasise the dire nature of the employment market in the UK. Many of the unemployed are from ethnic minorities. The way the unemployed were presented was to suggest that they are victims of a failed economy. Many complain that they have written dozens of CV's but are rarely interviewed. It is evident that these complainants are likely to engage in self-employment but are likely to also be long-term unemployed. They continue to complain and to become disenfranchised members of society as the benefit screw tightens.

The systems of control are of course developed by politicians often in order to pursue their own peculiar ideas and preferences. Who would have thought that the post Second World War notion of providing refuge for asylum seekers following Hitler's Holocaust would result in uncontrolled mass immigration. In yet another dispatches programme on Channel 4 on 15 April 2013 journalists obtained inside information about the running of the Border Agency. As John Reid pointed out many years ago the then Home Secretary, the border agency was "not fit for purpose". We saw chaos in the programme with senior managers ducking and diving in order to avoid their responsibilities. We saw the figures being manipulated and details missing in order to confuse and mislead politicians who are responsible for the safety and security of the U.K.'s borders. It appears that Theresa May's 2013/4 well-intentioned scrapping of the agency status of the border agency was little more than a cosmetic makeover.

It became clear in the programme that the system was totally out of control and that thousands of students who had overstayed their visas were untraceable. The issue of knowing who is in the country and who was leaving again became a prominent issue. It is clear that people come into the country but are not recorded as leaving. It is therefore possible that thousands who are believed to be in the country are not or alternatively thousands who are believed to have left the country are still here lying low operating below the radar in the black economy.

We have seen the offspring of first-generation immigrants who are British born committing or attempting to commit the most appalling acts of terrorism too numerous to mention comprehensively. In the early part of 2013 we see four Islamic men from Luton convicted of planning to blow up targets in the UK, notably a territorial army base under whose front gates they planned to send a motorised toy carrying a bomb.

At the end of April 2013 we saw six Asian men plead guilty to plotting a terrorist attack on a rally organised by the English Defence League. These men arrived at the location of the rally after the event had dispersed due to its leader failing to attend. Fortuitous disorganisation as it turned out because these Islamic men were carrying illegal weapons including a makeshift bomb. Closed circuit television recorded them wandering about in the square from which the rally had dispersed. It was only good fortune that these would-be terrorists were apprehended when during their departure from the scene of the intended attack their car was stopped by the police having identified it as being uninsured.

Are these events carried out by 'British nationals' really the actions of British nationals proud of their identity bestowed upon them by a generous tolerant people? These tolerant people, having brought about their own potential demise sit back and do nothing. The Daily Express reported on 2 May 2013 that the white indigenous British will be a minority in the whole of the UK by 2066. Is this the reasonable fate of a tolerant generous people?

One of the consequences for the indigenous population of this mass immigration in addition to the violence wrought upon their streets by various gangs and factions is the call by the current Home Secretary Theresa May for the enactment of a communications bill, commonly known as a snooper's charter. This would allow the 'authorities' to listen in to telephone calls and look at the content of emails and texts as a matter of routine. This would be a massive infringement of long fought for rights and privacy.

In relation to the right to freedom of speech there were establishment attacks on this right when we examine the Julian Assange case. Assange the WikiLeaks founder having sought political asylum in the Ecuadorian Embassy in London faced instant arrest should he step outside by the numerous Metropolitan police officers on duty round-the-clock for that purpose. The estimated bill to 31/ 3/13 for the Metropolitan police presence being in excess of £3 million.

On 24 April 2013 three Islamic men were convicted of planning terror attacks on Wootten Bassett. This town recently receiving Royal status following its role in the disembarkation of deceased troops en route to their home towns or families. One of the convicted was a British white male being a recent convert to the Islamic faith.

In May 2013 professor David Coleman of Oxford University published a paper, one of many papers subsequently quietly forgotten and ignored. The title of the paper 'Migrants to change UK forever: White Britons 'will be in minority by 2066'. Britain will be the Western world's most ethnically diverse nation after 2050, according to this explosive academic study. Professor Coleman said migration has become the "primary driver of demographic change". It lays bare the effect of decades of immigration and claims that white Britons will be in a minority by 2066. A mass influx of migrants has given the UK the fastest-rising percentage of ethnic minority and foreign-born populations. The report which also reveals the huge impact of Labour's open-door policy to immigration between 1997 and 2010 – says foreigners and non-white Britons living here will double by 2040 and make up one third of the UK population.

On 9 May 2013 we note that two black men were convicted of manslaughter. Their victim an 85-year-old partially sighted lady was pushed over to rob her. Does this happen in South Africa, Nigeria, Russia? In general the answer is possibly yes but the context of many of these crimes no. Almost certainly the only country in the world which its politicians have voluntarily committed to a population of different races, tensions and cultures is Britain.

After a carnival in Luton on 26 May 2013 a stabbing occurred on the 27th. The carnival being a gay affair with many ethnic minorities performing in very colourful costumes followed by such a sad crime involving the stabbing of an individual apparently by two black males and a female. Police were appealing for witnesses.

In the latter part of May 2013 we witnessed, literally, on our TV screens the aftermath of the running down of soldier, drummer Lee Rigby the outside Woolwich barracks in London. He was attacked subsequently by two black men of Nigerian descent born in Britain apparently with the intention of hacking him to death and removing his head! These two men were apprehended by police after they had given interviews to passers-by apparently with the intention of seeking publicity with regard to their 'Islamic' struggle! One of these men apparently raised in South London of a "devoutly Christian family" and a recent convert to Islam was it is alleged approached by MI5 with a view to becoming a British spy! Woolwich subsequently witnessed an outpouring of grief by the British public and the place where Rigby was hacked to death has become a shrine.

On the weekend following the Rigby murder the English Defence league marched in London to protest about the Islamic faith, variously being described as the 'far right' or 'yobs' simply out to 'cause trouble'. Following this disgraceful attack in broad daylight on Rigby some 180 reprisal attacks in various forms have allegedly been made on Islamic people and their religious establishments. This behaviour on both sides is clearly based on tribal instincts and is little influenced by the possible consequences. Two British men were arrested for their part in allegedly attacking a mosque followed by the hand wringing of many politicians prepared to condemn for what is arguably normal behaviour in the circumstances.

The Lee Rigby case and many others appear to be a clear demonstration that the integration of different tribes and cultures in general simply does not work. There is a clear and arguably natural dislike of those of different cultures and religious practices. This condemned as racism. One has only to look at English history dating back to the Tudor times in relation to the conflicts between the Catholic Church and the English to understand the delicacy of social equilibrium.

Assange previously referred to is trying to avoid extradition to Sweden on charges related to sexual assault/rape. The WikiLeaks founder published items on the internet certain actions by the United States government including footage of a United States helicopter gunship firing on 'civilians' in Pakistan, alleged to be connected with or actually being terrorists themselves.

Immigrants invariably choose us and not us them. They come here for a better life and who is to blame them? Have British politicians been too generous or too stupid? Whilst the Labour Party was in power between 1997 and 2005 there is no doubt that the then Prime Minister's Blair and Brown respectively both had open door policies and a complete lack of control which led to mass immigration. The British were told that they would have long days in retirement funded by the hard-working immigrants who would enrich their lives?

The British were also told these people are needed to do the jobs the British don't want in either agriculture, the NHS, catering, transport and other fields. Were these deceitful lies? The maxim of some 'never trust a politician', they seek only to tell you what they think you want to hear and rarely are they held accountable for the lies they spin and the long term difficulties they cause.

It may be somewhat melodramatic to suggest that the British and particularly the English are spectators en route to their own funeral procession since it is estimated by Prof David Coleman of Oxford University, see above; that the white British will be a minority in Britain by 2066. This alarming forecast is not pie in the sky. It cannot be doubted given the birth rates of the immigrant population as compared with those of the indigenous community.

Noting that many towns and cities by 2015 already have a majority immigrant population and that some immigrants have taken control of certain areas and postcode gangs terrorise and control the streets by killing and stabbing their so-called adversaries. These gangs are invariably comprised of minority ethnic groups. The British have become onlookers in their own downfall with the authorities unable to control the population, the country at large or its finances.

It is evident that if the English were less accommodating and more aggressive then there would be civil war on the streets and it is with dark foreboding one may visualise such events transpiring in England as the various factions vie for power. A fine example of shooting oneself in the foot, practiced many times by the British government; is the matter of the Afghan interpreters 600 of whom were given right to settle in the UK in 2014. This must surely include their families where appropriate and we all know of course this will be at the taxpayer's expense and the Afghans have large families. Were we not in Afghanistan interfering in a sovereign country this would not be an issue to address. So what 600 here or there? Well it's another 600, another drop in the overflowing bucket.

On 14/10/13 we saw the Home Secretary Theresa May making political noises and gestures as to the need to control immigration and then contradicted wholesomely by George Osborne who on a trade visit to China announced the relaxation of visa allocations to the Chinese at large.

On 16/10/13 we saw on the BBC News that thousands of girls are being exploited sexually and abused by gangs in London and England in general. In a news item the same week we saw the BBC reporting on the illegal trafficking of 'slaves' into the UK many of which are from East European countries. Yes slaves!

The BBC in its Panorama programme on 28/10/13 noted that there had been a 20% increase in the British population since the 1960s with a corresponding <u>500%</u> increase in rubbish and litter being left in the streets. Is there a connection or is this a no-brainer?

On 3 April 14 the BBC News reported that there had been a 75% increase in type II diabetes with Afro-Caribbean and other ethnic groups three times more likely to get the disease. The cost of treating these imported diseases is huge and a further burden on the British taxpayer.

On 13 April 14 we see the BBC news reporting on benefit cuts which are affecting many families. These benefit cuts amount to a cut on benefits payable at the rate of £500 per week or more. Noting that this sum is a figure that many hard-pressed families can only dream of, we see an Indian couple, neither of whom are employed; with five children complaining about the prospect of having to move out of a high cost rental area to reduce costs to equal to or less than the new £500 per week cap. It is not only inconceivable that this state of affairs should exist but beyond belief that these circumstances are not at all uncommon.

On 6 May 2014 a Channel 4 news report included comments from a 'British man' with Eritrean roots. This man made it clear that he resented being called British although he had grown up in Britain. He was quite resentful about a number of issues and made it quite clear that in his view Britain owed the world for what it had done. He was referring to Britain's past colonial days in particular but more importantly was referring to the international role we take unto ourselves at present. This man's views are clearly not uncommon within the ethnic population and taken to the extreme manifest themselves in violence, example the death of Lee Rigby.

On the same day 6/5/14 we noted that the latest government forecasts suggest that ethnic minorities who are currently around 15% of the population is forecast to be around 30% in 2050. There is clearly a divergence between this forecast and substantial pieces of previous research including Prof David Coleman's of Oxford University which stated that white people will be a minority in the UK by 2050. Could it possibly be that the British government are understating the impact of immigration upon the UK? Surely not?

On 12 May 2014 the BBC Panorama programme reported on the prison population currently at around 85,000 inmates. The program stated that in the last 10 years ethnic minority prisoners have doubled in the UK to 12,000 and consequently they comprise one in seven of the prison population.

Somewhat more alarming in relation to the prison population is the high security prison at Whitemoor of which some 40% of its population are Muslims. Do these statistics indicate a relatively high degree of disrespect for the laws and people of the host country by Muslims?

On 17 May 2014 we see a further expose of immigration test centres falsifying results for the English test required for immigrants to enter the UK. We noted that some applicants didn't actually attend the test centre at all but upon production of £500 in cash were permitted to pass the English test. Mr James Brokenshire - Immigration Minister made the usual political noises in relation to investigating the matter, fraud etc.

On the 27 May 2014 BBC News reports that Tower Hamlets voting papers were still being counted after most other boroughs had completed the count. With concerns that large numbers of Asian men have been gathering outside numerous inner-city polling stations in London police were stationed outside the stations to prevent Asian men allegedly attempting to influence or intimidate voters in relation to their voting intentions.

On 27 May 2014 we note that the BBC News reports that liver disease is the fifth biggest killer and rising in the UK. We also note that liver disease together with numerous others is prolific amongst the ethnic minority communities at a substantial cost to the population at large.

On the 28th of May 2014 news reports refer to a Pakistani woman being stoned to death in an honour killing outside the High Court in Pakistan. Police and the public are seen to be standing by as the killing occurred. The killing was carried out by the woman's family. She was five months pregnant by a man to whom she had not been promised or more precisely 'arranged' to be married to. We also note that this was occurring as a number of rapes were also occurring in India the victims then being hanged by the neck from trees. This is not an unusual occurrence in India and is of particular concern to women in the lower castes.

At the end of May 2014 we note that the British government intends to make illegal a drug imported by the Somali and Yemeni communities, the Yemen coincidentally being on the brink of civil war. This green 'vegetation' drug 'Khat' has hallucinogenic powers and was not banned for fear of upsetting ethnic minority communities. No doubt this and the many other activities of ethnic minorities are considered to be an enrichment of the lives of the indigenous population by the politicians and the BBC who continue to portray an abundance of mixed race relationships on publicly funded television stations.

At the beginning of June 2014 we note that London gangs number 240 with an estimated 3000 members the majority of whom (77%) are allegedly from ethnic minorities.

On 2 June 2014 the BBC reported on hundreds of would-be migrants to England in Calais. The squalid camp that they occupy being cleared by the police because of disease. The stated destination of the migrants being England "the promised land" Most of them speak English in varying degrees of fluency and already have relatives in the UK. Mass immigration into the UK is now so endemic that each immigrant community now acts as a Trojan horse for new immigrants be they legal or otherwise.

On 3 June 2014 Channel 4 reports on a series of substantial raids in the UK by the immigration authorities in relation to illegal workers. These raids being carried out by the Home Office had been sabotaged by an internal leak to the target businesses, when officials arrived at the target addresses any illegal immigrants had long since gone. So, we have both a Trojan horse effect and the 'enemy within'.

On the subject of the enemy within we saw John Snow on Channel 4 News introducing a number of young females who had taken the initiative to use the 'You Tube' social media network to advertise some lifestyle products, cosmetics etc. Snow commented at the end of the piece that they all looked white and middle-class. Krishnan Guru Murthy, Snow's co-presenter, couldn't resist a snigger. Perhaps he thought that Snow's apparently derogatory comment as to the race of the girls was amusing? Perhaps he was astounded that a white man should make such remarks? This is not an unusual state of affairs and needs to be considered further, Greg Dyke as director general of the BBC once remarked that the BBC was 'awfully white' implicitly lacking ethnic minorities.

What is it that makes a person turn on their own kind? Is it self interest, political correctness or are they simply traitors? It is certainly 'unusual' that a member of one ethnic group should hold in such disdain his/her fellow members.

In the meantime on 16 June 2014 we noted that forced marriages were made illegal in the UK. This includes anyone wishing to send a female abroad to be forcibly married to a foreign national. This practice prevalent in the Pakistani community within the UK who also practice the medically unsound idea of marrying cousins which gives rise to many expensive to treat medical conditions.

We note that the 'enrichment' of British lives by ethnic minorities includes a high incidence of domestic violence, forced marriage, observance of the mediaeval Sharia law, female genital mutilation, the killing of animals without first stunning them and other unsavoury and arguably uncivilised practices.

We noted a report on 24 June 2014 that an estimated 50,000 immigrants have illegally entered the country via bogus English language tests exposed in a BBC Panorama programme. Some 54 London colleges were involved in cheating across five campuses. Given the slack if not total lack of attention that the government pays to immigration a reasonable person may assume from observations in and around the capital that this estimate of 50,000 is probably very underestimated. It is quite evident that many ethnic minorities of working age do not entertain the possibility of honest work and as such are supported by the generous British people.

We see on 24 July 2014 that Nick Griffin has been ousted from the leader's position he has held in the BNP (British National Party) invariably reported as a far right group for many years and has now been appointed its president. This follows the loss of Griffin's European Parliament seat in the last European elections. It appears evident that even the BNP has finally had enough of Griffins poor leadership and defensive, incoherent lack lustre ramblings.

In contrast to the downfall of Griffin BBC News continues to report on the various religious schools in Birmingham which are reported as having "an aggressive Islamic ethos" and had been taken over it is reported by a group who were "promoting hard line Islamic views". This all sounds fairly innocuous on paper except that for those of us who know Birmingham and similar cities particularly the inner-city areas of those conurbations will understand that many of them now appear to be part of an Islamic state rather than English cities.

We have all been made aware in recent years that those who employ illegal immigrants face stiff fines. Many will remember the trial of a prominent politician in relation to the employment of an illegal immigrant. In more recent times we heard on 23 July that Mark Harper the former immigration minister's ex-cleaner had been detained in Yarlswood detention centre awaiting deportation to Colombia. She was naturally very sad about this state of affairs having been in the UK doing a job of work for many years. She asserts that during seven years work for Mr Harper she was not asked to demonstrate she was in the country legally. Moreover it appears she had produced a forged letter allegedly from the Home Office granting her leave to remain. Mark Harper who refused to comment on the matter has now 'reappeared' as a government Minister in the Department for Work and Pensions. It is tempting to suggest that the most seriously incompetent ministers should be put to work in the Home Office since no further damage can be done in that department.

On 26 July 2014 we see in the news broadcasts that Greg Dyke, former director-general of the BBC and now chairman of the football Association has pronounced that the council of this organisation is 'overwhelmingly white and male'.

This 'Englishman' has not for the first time denounced his countrymen in favour of some politically correct positive discrimination towards ethnic minorities. Whilst at the BBC he made similar pronouncements and it is apparently his intention to rearrange the membership of the Council of the Football Association as is the case at the 'left wing' BBC. He holds that English players are however in shortage.

Dyke's pronouncement follows the recent pronouncement of the Commissioner of the Metropolitan police in suggesting that the police force in London should reflect the ethnic mix of London. Neither of these pronouncements addresses the question of suitability, indigenous sensitivities as to their own culture, aptitude or the propensity of ethnic minorities to be relatively disrespectful of the law, culture and customs of the indigenous population.

A major question that arises from this discussion is why the English feel so inadequate and feel the need to be so 'politically correct' so as to commence on the path to their own destruction. Can it be that this highly regulated relatively docile, civilised society has over the years been so controlled by its political 'masters' that is afraid en masse to speak up or even appear 'racist'? The word racist is of course applied as a derogatory term to the damned, ie; anyone who should even appear to be anti-foreigner. Those of us who are a bit longer in the tooth can remember that the British were well known for their dislike of 'Johnny foreigner' often for good reason.

In the first week of August 2014 to the astonishment of many people in the UK the authorities have established a free phone help line in order to abolish what they call 'Modern Slavery' in the UK. Modern slavery it appears has several forms and can include people trafficked to the UK to perform prostitution under the control of pimps, illegal immigrants being forced to do household work for their hosts without pay, people kept as virtual prisoners and forced to work etc. Who would have thought this even possible 50 years ago?

On 1/8/14 the Daily Telegraph reports on uncontrolled immigration and the impact it is likely to have on hospitals and water shortages. It refers to a 20 million growth in the population over the next 50 years if immigration continues at the current rate. The article is based on a report from 'Civitas' and refers to the net inflow of migrants as 200,000+ per year despite the government of the day's avowed intention to reduce this to tens of thousands by 2015. The achievement of this target the report concludes is impossible. The author is reported to have said "unrestrained population growth would eventually have a negative impact on the standard of living through its environmental effects such as overcrowding, congestion and loss of amenity." We have all seen the pictures on television of the crowded streets of Pakistan and some of us may have seen similar scenes on the Stratford Road in Sparkhill, Birmingham. Is this really best for the country?

On 16 August 2014 a container ship is unloaded at Tilbury docks in East London and shouting and screaming is heard from the inside of one of the containers. 35 people from the Indian subcontinent are found to be inside the container one of whom is dead. They are found initially to be suffering from hypothermia and dehydration. It appears that they had been trafficked to the UK, the chosen destination of most 'developing country' immigrants. The occupants of the container are treated humanely despite the obvious language difficulties and initially dispatched to various hospitals in the London area to receive healthcare. If this kind of illegal immigration was occasional then there would be little cause for alarm but the truth is that there is a steady flow of illegal immigrants and a steady flow of legal immigrants thus creating an unsustainable burden on the country into the future.

We can deduce from the various snapshots cited above that the settled population is burdened with huge costs arising from all forms of immigration. A number of cases are known to the author where members of the indigenous population are being squeezed out of their local communities by immigrants to whom subsidies are often made in the form of Council Tax relief by the established population. This is called redistribution or should we now say to be politically correct 'progressive' taxation.

On the matter of taxation and the burden of costs we note there on 18 August the so-called 'e' border security system commissioned by the Labour government in 2007 at a cost of £750 million has been scrapped. The system which it was intended would register immigrants and emigrants from the country did not work. The cost of cancellation alone to the taxpayer amounts to £234 million. The Daily Mail provided information suggesting that approximately 20% of all travellers through UK Borders were unaccounted for.

We note Sky News reports on 17 August 2014 that 18,000 illegal immigrants were detained in the UK in 2013 and that Global News reports on 20 August 2014 that some 50+ trafficked persons are discovered every week in Britain. 1000's set sail in unseaworthy boats from the north coast of Africa every month to reach Europe.

Who can doubt that government is failing in Britain, failing in its most fundamental duty to protect its people and control its borders? The public hear little of use from the Home Secretary Theresa May or any senior figure from the 'unfit for purpose' Home Office. On 26 August 2014 a further 13 illegal immigrants have been found in the back of a truck and having reached their destination will no doubt be making successful applications for asylum and further increasing the burden on the taxpayer.

On 26 August 2014 a report by Professor Alexis Kay is published regarding the abuse of children in Rotherham between 1997 and 2013. The report that concludes some 1400 cases of physical, mental and sexual abuse have occurred under the noses of the police and social services of Rotherham Council. The abuse which includes the gang raping of girls under the age of consent, physical abuse and in one case a young person was doused in petrol and threatened that they would be set on fire if they did not comply with the abuser's orders. Girls as young as 11 were the report states trafficked between councils, raped and beaten and terrorised as recently as 2013. This was despite several previous reports drawing the authority's attention to the matter. The abuse has been systematically carried out by members of the Pakistani community in both Rotherham and other towns throughout England. One of the shocking aspects of the case is that the local police and council had disregarded complaints from the abused in the so-called interest of community relations. Not one single person at the date of report had been disciplined.

It is estimated that there are 2 million Muslims in Britain a proportion of whom have declared their hatred for their host country Britain and gone to fight as 'jihadis' in Syria and Iraq. A further proportion carry out the abuses that we see outlined above.

On 28 August 2014 we note that four black men were convicted of murder and manslaughter at the Old Bailey. They killed a 24-year-old white male Dean Mayley in broad daylight. Dean was stabbed in the heart by one of the black men. It appears the motive was robbery. The victim was probably confused when he was attacked since he had the mental age of nine and was described as a mild, polite young man. The victim subsequent to the trial was also described as one of the nicest young men one could wish to meet. His parents and relatives were naturally distraught at this pointless loss. More 'enrichment' of England's culture!

On 4 September 2014 a black man was arrested after an elderly woman was found beheaded in a garden in North London. On the same day more than 80 would-be illegal immigrants were caught on camera evading the French police at the port of Calais in order to get on ferries or any other form of transport bound for England, 'the promised land'.

By September 2014 we saw huge numbers of people needing accommodation and the country's graveyards full to bursting particularly in London. Consideration was being given to recycling grave spaces over 75 years old such is the shortage of space in general. This idea would have been inconceivable 50 years ago. As one official put it this would be "breathing new life into cemeteries". When he made this statement his face was without expression; one might say dead pan.

As immigrants continue to flood into the country unchecked we learned in late September 2014 that a teenage girl has gone missing in London and a Latvian man seen on CCTV had disappeared. The Latvian man was sought by the police and it appeared had a record including the murder of his wife in his homeland Latvia. It further transpires that no checks whatever are made on immigrants from the European Union as to their criminal pasts other than the most naive questions at the border of the individual themselves. The girl and suspect were later found dead.

The mass immigration from Eastern Europe continues and Romanian gangs are engaged in the organisation of substantial numbers of sham marriages allegedly for gay people. These sham marriages are said to account for between 20 and 30% of all marriages in the UK and are carried out for no other reason than to acquire papers in order to become resident in the UK. Each sham marriage costs approximately £10,000 such is the high value of a UK passport. These events are indicators of the gross incompetence of the Home Secretary's Department at The Home Office which remains unfit for purpose.

On 19 September 2014 we noted that the Scottish referendum held on the 18th declares that Scots have voted to remain within the UK and do not wish to be an independent country. We saw the un-statesmanlike spectacle in the closing stages of the campaign of England's politicians entering into a bidding war to bribe the Scots to remain in the union. This was despite most polls indicating that the Scots would vote no to independence in any event. The inducements offered to the Scots will be shown in turn to cost the UK dear, not least the English who had no say whatever in the referendum. We further noted that the Scottish economy is heavily subsidised by England under the ongoing burden of the Barnett formula which enables greater public funds to be spent on the Scots then is spent on those who pay for it, the English.

As diseases such as the Ebola virus and malaria sweep through Africa and wars in the Middle East expand geographically, masses of immigrants flood the country without let or hindrance. Some medical volunteers return to the UK with the deadly virus!

How could the arrogant, incompetent British government over so many years hold their own people in such contempt that such a punishment as their eventual extermination should be visited upon them? For the time being those in office look down their noses with contempt upon the English reminiscent of post the Norman conquest in 1066.

Chapter 16

Religion

Religion in a secular society is a highly contentious area. Is this a provocative suggestion? Doubtful! Religion appears to consist of a belief or series of beliefs in some form of being, deity or idea, that form having espoused some sort of doctrine which encourages people to follow the said doctrine. There are many doctrines. Some appear to be harmless, some appear to be harmful and quite aggressive. The Romans as pagans had many gods as do some societies today. Some appear to place high status on usually male believers in a community and some appear to encourage strict forms of corporal and occasionally capital punishment for what some Western civilisations believe to be relatively trivial matters.

Britain has seen many races apparently encouraged to settle in the UK. These foreigners, who the indigenous population were traditionally highly suspicious of; have brought with them a rich tapestry of behaviours and beliefs. These include the importation of witchcraft and a relatively recent case has identified the serious implications of such beliefs i.e. the discovery of a headless torso of a young black person in the River Thames. In addition, it appears that slavery is alive and well not only in the UK but also in other parts of the world. Does Britain have enough existing problems to deal with?

Our politicians without reference to the population at large make decisions that have far-reaching effects on the country and society. They get elected and as we all know power corrupts, absolute power corrupts absolutely. Give a political party a majority and there is no limit to the daft ideas that they will conjure up and impose on the population. It appears meddling politicians who wish to impose their ideas on the population cause major disruption and later decide there is a problem and proclaim they can fix it. They then set about screwing up the solution at great expense. There is no consistency as Britain lurches from centre-left to centre-right. The politicians 'dance on pinheads' to appeal to the maximum number of voters. Do we get what we deserve?

So what if a troublesome man got himself crucified 2000 years ago? He may have been a good man, he may have been self-sacrificing, well-intentioned and very kind to his mother and old ladies. The Roman rulers of the day thought he was undermining their authority. It is difficult to believe given the fiction found in the Bible about the creation of the heavens and the earth in six days, that the claims as to Christ's miracles also are not exaggerated. Even if there was such a man it is beyond the rational to <u>worship</u> such a legend. Why not worship Robin Hood? We see the damage that such worship can do in the alleged misappropriation of Islamic ideals and the disgraceful behaviour of priests particularly apparently those of the Catholic persuasion.

No man is an island, however to divest oneself of personal and intellectual integrity to be subsumed by this or that religion is arguably primitive. In modern society we hold in disdain witch doctors and the like spreading their personal influence and power through juju and other strange beliefs. The extraordinary consequences of criticising others irrational religious beliefs is however a force to be considered noting that Salman Rushdie was sentenced in absentia to death for his authorship of The Satanic Verses.

Some have suggested that the Islamic faith is bringing a revival of religion to the UK. This appears to suggest that religion is universally a good thing. To some an affront to the rational is the attempt to suggest that life under the influence of religious zealots practising beliefs invented 500 years or more ago would be in improvement on our current situation. Well it may be to some but to many others a return to the religious fervour of the past would be a betrayal of modern thinking and highly regressive; remember the inquisitions. We have seen the religious despots controlling our lives for long enough. Some may recall it prior to the beginning of the second world war when Archbishop Cosmo Gordon Laing was instrumental in obtaining Edward VII's abdication in 1936. We see in this Archbishop the zealous power of the clergy.

In March 2013 the world witnessed the election of a new Pope from the conclave of Cardinals gathered in the Vatican City. Pope Francis an apparently good man from Argentina will lead the world's 1.2 billion Catholics. These people hold a set of beliefs including the sanctity of life. This prohibits the use of contraceptives and is therefore contributing to an ever-growing world population, many of whom are unable to feed themselves. How can it be that a group of men who have taken a vow of celibacy and include amongst their number paedophiles and child abusers that they should have the arrogance and hypocrisy to suggest that they have any moral compass from which to guide the populous from any point of view? The answer, many people need some form of direction, they need some external strength to get through life, strength that is not manifest in their own selves and character.

Towards the end of March 2013 we noted that the former Archbishop Dr Carey accused the coalition government in the UK of 'aggressive secularism'. One wonders whether the established church or the Catholic Church or the Islamic faith, the Jewish faith or something else should replace secularism? Totalitarian belief?

On 22 April 2013 Panorama a well-known investigative news programme on BBC investigated Sharia councils in Britain which are acting as quasi judicial bodies in relation to those that wish to submit to them or are obliged to for example by 'marriage'. Panorama found that these councils which have great influence in the Islamic community are very male biased and exercise what is effectively an Islamic common-law which may also be termed Islamic preferences and protocols. There is little protection for women under Sharia law which is dominated by men.

On 20 May 2013 the formerly 'straight' Church of Scotland voted to except gay clergy! This landmark decision will affect the church forever. Westminster MPs on the same day were debating allowing gay marriage. The extraordinary consequences of these decisions by politically correct minded people is quite extraordinary when one considers that religion whose doctrine has been accepted for 2000 years and is based on the teachings of Jesus Christ, can be overturned on a comparative whim. That the state should impose its will into a religious matter, albeit marriage is a form of contract and aggrieved parties can and often do seek redress against their ex-spouses in the courts; is quite beyond belief. The state is clearly creating a new definition for marriage.

At the end of May 2013 we saw a Pakistani International Airways jet escorted to Stansted by RAF jets the pilot having declared an emergency en route from Pakistan. We subsequently witnessed the spectacle of two Pakistani men or 'British' men being arrested and charged with putting the plane in danger. These men are alleged to have threatened to blow up the aircraft. On the same day we see the stabbing of a young ethnic minority person in Luton. Members of 'the community' being interviewed and of course explaining they don't understand why such things are occurring.

In September and October 2013 we see the new Archbishop of Canterbury Dr Justin Welby proclaiming that we will put out of business certain commercial concerns lending money at high rates of return. He then pronounces on 20/10/13 that the energy companies must look to their consciences in relation to the ever-increasing costs of fuel. Political comment from the clergy?

In the second week of December 2013 the Supreme Court of England held that the Church of Scientology is a church and not a cult and therefore persons may be married by that church. The status of becoming a church does of course convey a number of benefits, not least significant tax breaks as a charity.

On the 10/12/13 we become aware that universities UK (UUK) has decided that universities throughout the country may segregate the sexes for lectures involving a religious dimension, e.g., Muslims meeting as a society at university for a lecture. This segregation of the sexes appears to be a form of apartheid and has occurred in the week in which the whole world it seems celebrated the life of Nelson Mandela who died at the age of 95.

On 14 April 2014 various news media reports 25, yes 25 schools in Birmingham are in 'lockdown'. This means that they are under investigation following some 200 alleged complaints as parents, teachers and governors were regarding the apparent takeover of school governance by Islamic zealots. Who among us can remember the cunning Greeks and the use of the Trojan horse to take the otherwise impregnable city of Troy? More importantly did any of us consider what mugs the Trojans were for accepting such a gift without close inspection? Such are the contradictions of life which may signal the downfall of a society; some are of course contrarily taught not to look a gift horse in the mouth!

On 18 April 2014 we note that British exports are up! Great Britain is now exporting home grown Islamic jihadist fighters to Syria. It was estimated that there were 20 dead already out of a total of 400+. These people are described as British nationals. Is this now a reflection on the state of affairs in Britain with worse to come? Does anyone feel ashamed to be called a British national?

The Western world is horrified to hear that a Sudanese woman has been sentenced to death because she refused to recant her Christian faith. She is also facing 100 lashes for adultery arising from a relationship with a Christian. The Islamic faith views anyone born an Islamic who adopts another religion (apostasy) to be committing a form of treason the sentence for which is death. The Islamic faith also considers an Islamic born woman married to a Christian to be adulterous and therefore worthy of the 100 lashes. Is this the kind of Britain society wants in the future? When Cameron and Miliband are long gone what fate will befall our grandchildren?

Many are predicting that Britain will become subject to the Islamic faith in due course, a caliphate. The likes of Nick Griffin, former leader of the British National Party until deposed in July 2014 were already warning about this prospect. To date Britain has largely ignored and derided these warnings, symptomatic of the proverbial ostrich with its head in the sand.

In May 2014 Sajeed Javed was appointed the new culture secretary. No this is not imaginary, a man with asian roots is the British culture secretary. Is this possible anywhere else in the world? Furthermore what does it say about the British culture or lack of pride in it?

On 18 May 2014 Mr Javed pronounced that migrants to Britain must speak English and respect the culture. We note that many immigrants to Britain particularly those from the subcontinent who have been in Britain for up to 50 years still do not speak English.

In June 2014 we note the number of schools in Birmingham, Luton and other cities are again being investigated for deploying an unsuitable curriculum designed to foster extreme Islamic views and behaviour. This behaviour including separation of the sexes in teaching and a narrow view of Islamic beliefs to the exclusion of any other religion or beliefs. On 9 June 2014 Park View and Golden Hillock schools in Birmingham are featured prominently in the news with Asian parents being interviewed. They show a suitable degree of surprise and indignation at the process of 'special measures'. Meanwhile a school in London was found to have terrorist related materials on the premises. Politicians wring their hands and state that they missed the warning signs.

In June 2014 the Olive Tree School in Luton is being exposed as being a repository for extremist materials including material suggesting that stoning and lashing are appropriate punishments. On the same day the Pakistani Taliban storms Karachi airport resulting in 27 deaths. No one publicly acknowledges that the world is at war!

On 10 June 2014 further concerns were expressed about Islamic extremism in a Bradford School. The Prime

Minister continues to stress the values of British Society which he contends must be maintained. This position appears to be vaguely reminiscent of the King Canute story the indigenous population were taught about as children. Canute had absolute power, Cameron has the power of a coalition government! The distinction, despite being academic, is that neither Canute nor Cameron could stem the tide. On the same day in Iraq the country's second-largest city falls into the hands of a terrorist Islamic group.

It was reported in July 2014 that boys in an East Birmingham school were being taught that wives must obey their husbands. This includes voluntary submission to the sexual demands of the men concerned. Schools are also being identified as indoctrinating their pupils in the belief that modern Britain is a bad and corrupt place. Furthermore a number of state funded Islamic and Jewish schools which include a number of illegal 'yeshivas' (teaching religion only) and excluding the theory of evolution as just a theory are exposed. More than 10 illegal schools have been found where pupils report very early in the morning and often leave very late at night after a days brainwashing.

Some Christian schools are also teaching a form of indoctrination in the denial of the theory of evolution in preference for the adoption of the proposition contained in the Bible that the world was formed in six days. On 14 July Channel 4 dispatches reported that some schools have banned clapping by way of applause and music. The idea here is that some religious groups will not allow anyone to be applauded as if they were gods and that music is a corrupting and inappropriate influence.

Channel 4 news on 14 July 2014 revealed that there are approximately 100 Sharia law courts operating in the United Kingdom. These so-called courts operate openly although they have no legal standing. They are unaccountable, unregulated and rather reminiscent in their operation of the mediaeval courts of England.

On 24 July 2014 we see general reports in the news that two sixteen year old sisters have left the country to provide support services to the insurgents in Syria and Iraq, or to be more precise ISIS (the Islamic State of Syria and Iraq) they have broadcast via social media that their brothers and sisters should shake off their desire for material possessions and come to Syria and Iraq to do the work of Allah. The work of Allah appears to be manifest in the triggering of a religious war between the Sunni and Shia sects of the Islamic faith. Recent estimates range from between 500 and 2000 people who have left the UK to fight as insurgents.

On 14 August 2014 the BBC News reported that the former rapper who lived in a council flat in Maida Vale, London one Asil Majeed Abdul Barry has appeared on Twitter triumphantly holding someone's severed head. This is by no means unique and is clearly designed to terrorise in the name of Allah. Having been welcomed into the country and given British passports we can claim that Jihad is one of Britain's growing export lines?

In 2014 we see the rise of believers in the Islamic faith in the UK. Politicians desperately try to convince the population that the 2,000,000+ Muslims in the UK are peaceful and law-abiding citizens. Muslim leaders themselves by and large denounce violence in the extreme forms of Islam, for the time being. The more aggressive Muslims, resentful of their decadent hosts; can't and probably won't wait for the formation of an Islamic state in the UK. It is just a matter of time before this growing population asserts its authority in the UK as it did in Syria and Iraq recently.

Chapter 17

Racism

Racism is held to be a very derogatory word when used as a descriptor of another person. It is not clearly defined but appears to suggest that the dislike of a person from another race is strictly taboo, unpleasant and shameful. And yet we must ask whether this is politically correct to the point of social conditioning? A brief review in the first chapter suggested that in our prehistoric past certain behaviours were key to survival and have become part of our ethnic characters over the years. In order to survive it was essential to be wary of ones neighbours since without law the risk of being killed, eaten or sacrificed was reality. Survival was paramount. Is it through these mechanisms that tribes developed a sense of community ergo 'racism'?

What is a community? In its basic form it is probably a grouping of people who have decided that to be in a group is more beneficial than to act as individuals. Is it wrong to dislike those from another tribe based on our primeval instincts? Is it wrong to be suspicious of those with a different agenda, different cultures and those that behave differently? Let us remember that most wars and conflicts arise from the desire to acquire territory or from religious beliefs and previous commentary suggests that religious beliefs must certainly fall into the category of irrational behaviours.

More than half of all violent crimes committed in the Metropolitan police area are committed by gangs and in the middle of March 2013 it was reported that 50% of all

London boroughs are seriously affected by gang violence. Whilst gangs are not new in Britain and some of us may recall the Kray's, the Great Train Robbery etc, the phenomena of postcode gangs comprising of mainly 'immigrant descendant' youth in substantial numbers is a disturbing societal development. These gangs or tribes invariably seek some form of territorial control or another's possessions. Operation Trident was set up by the Metropolitan police some years ago specifically to address gun crime committed by black people. This turbulent sea of crime appears to swirl about the English as they attempt to go on with their normal daily lives and look on in disdainful passive amusement! Or do they?

Would it be racist to suggest that black ex-gang members or any gang member of any hue are inappropriate recipients of an OBE? Would it be racist to suggest that immigrants are choosing to settle here rather than the indigenous population choosing them to settle in the country? Any member of the EU may come to Britain to settle and work. Somalis, Africans, Asians, Russians, you name it, they're all in England. The number of garden sheds used as dwellings in the South West London area is rapidly increasing as a desirable means of low-cost accommodation without the burden of Council tax. If local councils clamp down as they threaten to do from time to time on these illegal dwellings then that same council will subsequently have a duty to re-house the occupants in them. The numbers are so vast this is clearly not going to happen and so the illegal immigrant living in someone else's garden shed is effectively protected by the state.

Is it racist to question the handouts in substantial sums in aid to foreign countries such as India, Pakistan who have invested heavily is nuclear weapons and the coffee growers in Ethiopia so that they may roast their own coffee? Why do we do it? Arrogant foreign secretaries have put it to us that this generosity is itself enlightened! That it prevents mass immigration. We see in the camp of immigrants at Calais that the Eritreans and Ethiopians hate each other and use the energy they have to fight amongst themselves. Tribes in action. Highly questionable policies or a lack of them are an admission that the government is not in control.

The English Defence League formed out of desperation it appears by the downtrodden English marched in support of the murdered drummer Lee Rigby on 27 May 2013 in the London streets. This movement, which does have some skinheads sporting uncouth tattoos, thereby providing evidence for those who wish to make derogatory comments, were vilified by a so-called antifascist movement for exerting their right to express themselves. The leader of the EDF Tommy Robinson, an Irishman apparently masquerading as English or so it would appear, receives hate mail and death threats frequently from it appears the Muslim population. 'Tommy Robinson' subsequently resigned for fear of persecution by ethnic minorities and joined the Quilliam Foundation!

In the run-up to the local council and European Parliament elections on 19 May 2014 we see Nigel Farage, leader of UKIP; being castigated by all news interviewers including Jeremy Paxman on Newsnight because of an unfortunate politically incorrect comment he made regarding the desirability of having a group of Romanian men as neighbours. Jeremy Paxman was at his pompous head boy best which included a sustained look of displeasure at Farage whose party continued to rise in popularity since it is the nearest party organisation to express the views of the common man as to immigration into Britain. Is the party racist? Does it matter?

The 31ˢᵗ annual British Social Attitudes Survey_of 3,000 people has revealed that a huge percentage of Britons - 95% - believe that in order for a person to be truly 'British' they must speak English, be born in Britain and have lived there for most of their life. Participators also believed (61%) that EU immigrants should have to wait three years before being able to claim benefits.

The study suggests Prime Minister David Cameron's hope to teach British values in schools might not be successful, as many people now believe 'Britishness' is something people must be born with and cannot go on to acquire in much the same way as the Chinese man can never be Indian.

The findings come as UKIP rides high in popularity after it topped the polls in the European elections and its leader Farage who campaigns for Britain to be politically independent from the EU was named Britain's most popular politician.

Wanting to be "truly British" whatever that means does not make one racist does it? In May 2014 a separate survey showed that one third of Britons stated they were racist, with one in three people admitting they regularly made comments or were involved in discussions which could be considered racist. Get over it, it's normal!

Gavin Sutherland, campaign coordinator for anti-racism educational group 'Show Racism The Red Card' stated "There are lots of people in this country who are proud to be British but that doesn't have to mean we are racist too. It is possible to separate the two. "It is possible to be patriotic and not racist, the 'Olympic effect' on attitudes in 2012 is a good example." The racist deniers are it appears abundant. Being racist does not mean denying one's own roots or hating other races does it? What does it mean? Is it a question of resources, overwhelming numbers, being swamped, loss of identity?

The survey, which has been run every year since 1983, found there had been a hardening of attitudes to immigration in the years 2004-14. The numbers of participants who believe that people must speak English to be British has gone up from 86% to 95%. The number of those who believe a Briton should have lived in the UK all their life to be British also rose six 6% in the past two decades to 77%.

English footballer Jack Wilshere gained support for his argument that in order to play for England a footballer should be born there and not be allowed to take advantage of FIFA's controversial "five-year residency requirement". He said: "If you live in England for five years it doesn't make you English." "The only people who should play for England are English people. If I went to Spain and lived there for five years, I'm not going to play for Spain."

Penny Young, chief executive of NatCen Social Research, agreed there had been a strengthening of hard line attitudes. She said: "In an increasingly diverse, multi-cultural country, we might expect people to be more relaxed about what it means to be British, yet the trend is going in the opposite direction. What is surprising about this comment is its inherent naivety as is the government's socially manipulative integration policy.

One might form the view in order to bring the matter into perspective that this small country England has absorbed a massive influx of aliens whose history is at a similar stage to that of England in the 12th or 13th century. Many will recall from history the horrors of the religious persecutions of the middle ages not least the belief in witches, trial by ordeal, the Spanish Inquisition etc. The notion of apostasy and any subsequent punishment that may follow such a 'crime' has become an everyday discussion point in recent years; hitherto rarely mentioned.

No one said the English, Welsh or Scots are perfect. The point is we are all entitled to be imperfect, others are entitled to be themselves and to live in their homeland without threat, let or hindrance as is the case asserted by every other nationality and indigenous people.

In August 2014 we see the separate killing of two black men in the United States. The first killing being in 'Ferguson' involving an allegedly armed young black man. Substantial rioting and looting followed. It must be noted that the police tribe comprises mainly white men. The aftermath continues.

Do forecasts suggesting that the indigenous population will be a minority by 2066 send a shiver down anyone's spine; those that may possess one anyway? This will be demographic ethnic cleansing by political correctness, stealth and incompetence.

Chapter 18

The Welfare State in Britain

After the massive losses of the country's young men in the first and second world wars the politicians of the day decided to create the 'cradle to grave' welfare state. This would mean free medical treatment for all no matter how wealthy or how poor the individual was. The National Health Service to provide whatever was needed. A land fit for heroes who paid for and deserved it. It is evident from these measures that this was socialism in its infancy. In the 1950s however life expectancy was limited and the system as it stood was unlikely to be a drain on the state. No one protested about the idea of 'to each according to their needs'. In the 1950s one could identify with one's neighbour as 'kith and kin'. This held notwithstanding the ancient and long established antipathy between the Irish and the English. There was no mass resentment in relation to the privileges and provisions of the welfare state.

It is an entirely different matter in the 21st century where the population of London has a majority of ethnic groups other than English. The indigenous population is outnumbered by foreigners in their own capital city. There are many other cities with large ethnic populations who in due course as the result of higher breeding rates will and in certain areas do already outnumber the indigenous population. No great statistical prowess is required in order to reach these conclusions other than a walk down any High Street in the suburbs of London, Birmingham, Leicester, Leeds and many others. The white man now includes huge numbers of Eastern Europeans, Poles Czechs, Russians, Latvians and the like are visible in many of Britain's towns and cities. No one can seriously doubt that Britain is both a soft touch and the final destination for many who seek new and better lives. This raises issues of fairness.

It is evident that foreigners coming to Britain from backgrounds which are impoverished both in education and financial terms. Thay are here to benefit from a fairly lax if not redistributive regime in relation to benefits and employment opportunities. Britain does not admit to positive discrimination. It is said that many employment opportunities arise from the unwillingness of the indigenous population to do menial jobs for low pay and whilst the benefits culture prevails the indigenous population will decline further in the land fit for heroes.

It appears undoubted that the welfare state has created a dependency culture. It will be interesting to see as time moves us all inexorably forward whether the 'visitors' on whom so much political capital has been vested will regress to the common denominator of dependency of which there is already some evidence. There is no money left, as Liam Byrne put it, to facilitate any further degree of dependency in the country. We shall see.

In January 2014 the rights under directive 2004/38 of the European Union applied to the Romanians and Albanians. These rights enable nationals of those countries to emigrate to any member state within the EU and after a short period of time to succeed to all the benefits and privileges of the nationals of those countries. In other words they can come to Britain and benefit the same as the indigenous population, the principle in the EU being equality.

It is said that these foreign nationals bring colour, new experience, new drive and enterprise in a country with an ageing population. It has previously been stated erroneously that they will pay for the pensions and increased leisure of the indigenous population. Never has such a political exaggeration been found to be so wanting. In 2013 it was noted that 27,000 of the 87,000 Rumanians already in the UK have been arrested. This is a huge overrepresentation by this segment of the population who are well known in London for their minor crime activities such as pick pocketing on the Tube and in contrast their major crime activities eg. trafficking of people. This human trafficking is often associated with a form of slavery and prostitution.

The welfare State of course includes many vestiges of socialism including subsidised social housing, Council owned properties and the like. Was it a co-incidence during the harsh economic climate following the financial crash that Lakanal House, a council block in central London, being refurbished in 2010 was not checked for compliance with Building Regulations and a subsequent fire in the block spread rapidly to a number of flats thus causing several deaths. It is reported that the fire service advised people in their flats to stay put. This turned out to be very bad advice for those that died.

One of many examples of the dysfunctionality and openness to corruption of the welfare state was, not for the first time broadcast on Channel 5 news on 17 April 2014 in their documentary programme entitled "How to get a council house". We saw a well organised immigration process bringing groups of Romanians and others to the UK. In order to qualify for the generous benefits, which all politically correct persons deny is their reason for travelling here; they arrive in the UK to be formed into groups by what might politely be called a gang master to go out into the community and collect scrap metal. They sell it to a scrap metal merchant who provides them with a receipt for the sale which in turn provides evidence that they are self-employed. This evidence of self-employment qualifies them as a 'worker' and automatically therefore entitles them to receive benefits in the host country. The benefits include council housing, jobseekers allowance etc. A person achieving 'worker' status in the EU sees the gates open to all host country benefits and host countries must not discriminate as to whether or not an applicant has made any contribution to the welfare system of the country.

No one doubted the sincerity of the Secretary of State for work and pensions Ian Duncan Smith at the time when he stated that he would like to offer the dignity of work to those on benefits. No one doubted his sincerity in attempting to establish the single benefits scheme. What was doubted, justifiably; was his ability to establish the necessary changes in order to turn the country around particularly within a minority coalition government. Watch this space.

In August 2014 we saw the government's Troubled Families Program sets new targets to help troubled families. The increase proposed was from the 120,000 to 500,000 families. It has been suggested that to the year 2014 the number of families who have made some substantial improvement is approximately 5000.

The welfare state in Britain it was estimated in 2012 spent approximately £23 million for translation services to immigrants. There is in 2014 a considerable debate about immigrants who do not speak the language and the burden they impose on the taxpayer. Many of them readily admit that they have made no effort whatever to speak the language over many years. Another self inflicted costly problem?

Chapter 19

The NHS

The National Health Service founded in 1947 employs over 1 million people in Britain. This huge organisation enjoys protection from economic reality at the highest political levels. It spends around £100 billion a year and is entirely taxpayer funded. In the early part of 2013 a report was published into the treatment of patients at Stafford Hospital. This hospital and others being highly criticised for its lack of care for its patients, moreover the goings-on at Stafford and other locations appear to resemble cruelty in some instances. This is not the NHS the population was promised after the hardships of the Second World War.

We are told that the immigrant population provides the backbone of many of our nationalised services and in particular the NHS. Some assert that the NHS and other services would collapse without immigrants. This is quite an extraordinary assertion when one considers that the immigrant population brings with it high levels of many diseases at a high cost to the NHS. Furthermore one cannot but gasp with incredulity when one hears of locum doctors applying to one region of the NHS and being rejected for their lack of language skills, subsequently applying to a different region in the NHS and being successful. It is further astonishing that this sacred cow the NHS appears to employ some doctors who have such an insufficient grasp of English that they neither understand their patients nor themselves are understood.

The Staffordshire report followed hotly on the heels of the scandals which have surfaced in private care homes where patients were abused, treated negligently or even assaulted. There is a problem which is that we very often encounter health-care workers from what used to be called the Third World administering services to the indigenous population. Services which we have seen often fall short of a reasonable standard.

Do we complain? Yes we do, but often it is too late. We cannot turn the clock back on immigration and we cannot turn the clock back when someone close to us dies through neglect or lack of care either at home or under the hospital system. The harsh truth is that we appear to care but not sufficiently to be effective nor to do anything about the decisions made by our politicians who were not elected to do things which cause most harm to the native population.

In 2013 it was suggested that not only do NHS staff not care, but that over 1100 people had been starved to death in the NHS system in the last two years. At the end of February 2013, a survey indicated that 50% of nurses in the UK think that their own concerns about patient care are ignored by their managers and senior staff. The NHS is not a free service. It costs around £100 billion of tax payers money per annum.

On 1/3/13 it was reported that breast cancer survival rates for the NHS were less than those in the equivalent organisation in Australia, Canada, Norway and Sweden. On 5 March 2013 The Lancet, a respected UK medical journal published by the medical profession reported that health outcomes in the UK had slipped to 14th position out of 19 compatible countries in relation to heart disease, cancer and blood pressure problems. Nonetheless we saw this sacred cow and its huge budget being protected by the then government. Is this appropriate, rational, good decision-making?

The Dispatches programme on Channel 4 reported in March 2013 on the Liverpool Care Pathway. This procedure involves end of life treatment or care or more precisely the lack of it. It is a process where the medical profession decide that a person's life is beyond cure or that a cure is beyond the realms of economic/medical capacity. This usually involves the elderly and entails the withdrawal of care for the underlying disease. The care provided is reduced to painkillers and sedatives. Is it too provocative to suggest that this is a step towards euthanasia but the procedure can include the withdrawal of food and drink. This is apparently often not explained correctly or fully to patients or relatives and arguably is a further infringement of a person's human rights, i.e. the right to life.

A Freedom of Information request revealed on 9 May 2013 that dozens of events occurring in the NHS were categorised as "never happen" events, eg, 7 inch long forceps being left in the abdomen of a patient. The patient in question gave an interview on the television news and was herself formerly a nurse. On 12 September 2013 the national news reports that NHS death rates are the highest in seven compatible countries in the Western world, the United States of America being one of them.

On 13 September 2013 we hear that ambulance crews are being sent on 999 calls without proper training and are therefore unable to administer even painkillers. This extraordinary state of affairs strongly suggests that the NHS is overfunded and out of control.

On 6/11/13 we hear that Colchester General Hospital has been falsifying cancer patient records in order to appear to be performing better than they are and on the 8/11/13 figures are published indicating that each baby costs the NHS £3700 of which £700 is spent by the NHS on negligence insurance. This is related to an increase of 80% in negligence claims over the last five years. Accompanying commentary suggested that the recruitment of additional midwives initiated by the baby boom has in turn been deemed necessary because of increasing birth rates arising mainly from immigration.

On 11 November 2013 we heard that a Dr Ian Patterson has been carrying out unapproved surgical procedures in Solihull and other hospitals which he calls 'cleavage sparing'. What this means in practice is that women with cancer are being offered partial mastectomy instead of the full mastectomy they need thus leading to a higher recurrence of cancer and subsequent death rates. This doctor also stands accused of carrying out unnecessary procedures for profit. Yet another NHS scandal, another cover-up?

On 19/11/13 for anyone in doubt as to the integrity of the NHS despite its 'protected' budget status within both the economy and the hearts and minds of the population Dr Jeremy Hunt – Secretary of State for health stated that 'cruelty had become normal in our NHS'. This fundamental revelation about the conduct of health service employees is quite staggering from a politician and its importance cannot be underestimated.

Was the NHS culture always cruel or is Hunt implying it has become so? If it has become so in recent years it is vital that we seek to understand why? This question is posed against the backdrop of the Staffordshire disgrace in the NHS and in many other parts of the organisation where patients are neglected and left to die. It is indicative of a system which is self perpetuating and to whom for many the patient is an inconvenience.

On 25/11/13 we note that the Channel 4 dispatches programme reports on the expanding costs of obesity to the NHS resulting from a huge increase in the last 20 years. This report coincided with the parallel news that young people today are surprisingly less fit than their parents.

On 4/ 12/13 we note that there is said to be a growing increase in response times for ambulances coupled with some ambulances being forced to wait outside hospital A&E departments before their patients can be admitted due to a lack of beds. When admitted some patients are obliged to wait on beds in corridors and the like. We are all familiar with queues in the UK and most of us are familiar with the idea queues can peak and decline rapidly. What we haven't seen historically in the UK is constantly increasing demand which can only be caused by an increasing population without a corresponding increase in capacity.

We note that on 10/12/13 Dr Berry, a surgeon operating in South Wales NHS has been suspended due to at least eight avoidable deaths. Dr Berry purports to be a liver specialist.

This short and not a comprehensive list of matters related to the NHS its performance and its people must oblige us to question the nature of change, the fabric and behaviour of society in this 'welfare state' which promised 'cradle to the grave care'.

On 18 April 2014 we see an NHS report indicating that foreign doctors are not as competent as those who are British trained. This is not a surprise since many of us have encountered doctors whose language and communication skills alone leave a great deal to be desired. Those doctors with what are deemed to be equivalent qualifications from any EU country may without challenge practice in the UK.

On 6 May 2014 the BBC News reports on the NHS and in particular asthma sufferers who are dying due to incompetent treatment.

On 11 June 2014 Channel 4 news reports on deaths not being reported to coroners in the NHS. Victoria Macdonald exposes the practice of failing to report infant deaths noting that only 'stillbirth' cases are not reportable. Remember the unauthorised use of body parts? Another NHS scandal?

On 17 June we note that the BBC reports that an enquiry in Scotland has revealed that the ashes of babies have been disposed of improperly without the knowledge of parents. Is this thoughtlessness, deliberate or malign? One might gain the impression that those in public service have presumed themselves to be above those they serve.

We note in June 2014 that there has been one death and several babies with the severe illness septicaemia resulting from an infected drip.

In June 2014 we hear that Crohn's disease has quadrupled in the UK and that the NHS budget of some £110 billion is at breaking point in some NHS trusts. Crohn's disease is a long-term condition that causes inflammation of the lining of the digestive system. Inflammation can affect any part of the digestive system, from the mouth to the anus. It most commonly occurs in the last section of the small intestine (ileum) or the large intestine (colon). It appears that such events are unsustainable.

On 16 August 2014 we see 34 illegal immigrants shipped off to join the queues at our hospitals in order to receive assessment and treatment courtesy of the British taxpayer on the NHS. Most of them if not all do not speak English and will be unable to say thank you, nor will they be able to pay since they have come to the shores in order to secure 'a better life' at Britain's expense.

In contrast in the first week of September 2014 we note that some cancer patients are being denied life prolonging drugs because they are said to be too expensive. In addition we note certain sectors dealing with the care of the elderly are castigated for delivering poor care with food in the NHS also being criticised for its unappealing nature and lack of nourishment. Should the reader need any further confirmation as to the perverse nature of priority setting in the NHS they may wish to note that the first hospital department in the NHS dealing exclusively with female genital mutilation (FGM) opened on 22 September 2014. FGM is a custom in many foreign countries and from the U.K.'s point of view is a further self inflicted burden, an exclusively imported problem for which the British taxpayer foots the bill.

Were we to control the way expenditure is allocated in the UK in general and government was less profligate we could provide a much higher standard of care in the NHS to those entitled to it, but it is far too late for that.

Chapter 20

The BBC

Recent times have seen a number of scandals at the BBC, a world wide renowned bastion of Britishness where a number of senior executives left the corporation, including George Entwistle the newly enthroned director-general. The scandals causing concern at the BBC included the Jimmy Savile saga and a number of other presenters who have been arrested and/or questioned over inappropriate conduct principally towards young ladies.

We see the BBC producing very expensive programs of which many are arguably of little use to mankind and a determination to spend their budget regardless of need. In a recent corporate move from London to Salford it is reported that dozens of staff were paid huge cost of transfer packages in sums exceeding £100,000.00. The BBC continues to broadcast worldwide and employs many niche/specialist reporters who focus on particular issues or a particular country. To the licence fee payer the payback is very little but this is again an example of an over bloated corporation publicising its own importance; a recognisably left-wing agent of the state.

The presenters, often sycophantic and with doubtful talent, often lack pronunciation skills and make annoying and patronising non-verbal gestures to their audience apparently because they cannot communicate without them. Few doubt that the BBC is a left-wing propaganda machine. The corporation reports on the most obscure matters and sends reporters all around the world often for the most trivial reasons and often when information can be gathered without travel at all. Viewers may have been surprised to hear on the 15/9/13 a feature length item on BBC1's Countryfile about trunk roads having tunnels dug under them to connect up door mouse populations. Bird boxes, a preoccupation with greater spotted newts, the protection of badgers and a variety of quite inane subjects are broadcast to the population at large most of whom care less.

The BBC does report on substantial items and many of their reports are unbiased and without favour. This is to the credit of the BBC who on 10/12/13 reported on the Newham college scandal of students being awarded course passes with little or no attendance. This college situated in East London refused to comment on this matter but as reporters dug into the issue it became apparent that some students names on the roll didn't exist at all. Is this reminiscent of the bogus colleges purporting to train foreign students whilst providing them with a backdoor entry system to the UK? Newham College was supported to the tune of £25 million per year by the tax payer.

On 10/12/13 we also hear from the BBC about the UK government's defence procurement activity which continues to waste prolific amounts of money in the billions together with the rail, universal credit system and almost any government activity you care to name. Let us not forget that in the second week of December 2013 an independent panel recommended a pay increase for MPs from £66,000 per annum to £74,000 per year, a whopping 11% increase! Even David Cameron was embarrassed by the size of this recommended increase when most of the population are seeing their purses squeezed by the largely foreign-owned energy companies.

On 11/12/13 we heard the shocking news from the office for standards in education (Ofsted) that white working class pupils are performing worst of all of any ethnic group in UK schools.

On 19 May 14 we see Joanna Gosling, a BBC News presenter interviewing Nick Griffin leader of the British National Party. The BBC's charter includes a requirement to be impartial, without this proviso we can only wonder whether they would choose to interview a person they describe as being on the 'far right' of British politics. The interview was typical of the BBC presenters in that it made every effort to belittle what many think are reasonably held views of the nationalists in relation to immigration and the effect the Islamic faith is having upon this supposedly Christian country. In a recent discussion with a warden in a Church of England setting in the rural and leafy valleys of Surrey he explained the greatest difficulty facing the church at the moment is declining congregations. He further explained that the congregation age group suggested that in 10 to 15 years there would be substantially less than the current 25% or so of Christian bottoms on seats.

On 2 June 2014 the BBC reported on the Jimmy Savile scandal. Such phrases as 'he hid in plain sight' and it 'says something about the nation' are used in Shelley Joffre's investigation. Savile abused patients at Broadmoor amongst many other institutions, was given keys to the establishment and was made head of the task force within the institution by the then Health Minister Edwina Currie. How can this possibly have occurred? Every observer the author ever discussed this with thought at the very least he was 'creepy'. Savile as at the beginning of June 2014 had attracted 500 complaints to the police and his abusive behaviour as a BBC presenter had been carried out over 60 years.

On 4 August 2014 we see a further ex-BBC radio one presenter admitting to numerous counts of sexual abuse at Southwark Crown Court with a trial pending on further charges.

On 21 August 2014 the BBC News features an Islamic presenter interviewing an Islamic contributor about Islamic terrorism. The interviewer conducts interviews in the street with Muslims. Unsurprisingly no English people are interviewed but then what is the point of asking rabbits their opinion on lettuce. The BBC presents other programs of a more balanced nature in order to spend its generous allocation of licence fee. This other reporting includes in August 2014 a sharp drop in English examination results in the London area.

It begins to appear that the BBC does foster bias and did allow a culture of molestation and sexual misbehaviour at its premises if only by its failure to apply proper standards and to act accordingly.

Chapter 21

A Future

Readers who have bravely made it to this page and have not succumbed to severe depression will be asking themselves whether the examples outlined above represent a country in terminal decline if not anarchy by the hand of government, if that is not a contradiction in terms?

People were asking at the general election in 2015 what are we to make of this apparent state of permanent chaos and muddle? No proper analysis in any depth of the dynamics of the UK, a country steeped in history and tradition with an indigenous population so loyal that they volunteered to fight for their country in the First World War and many did so in the Second World War. It is reasonable to suggest that the naturally inventive and creative nature of the indigenous population of Britain had been worn down by the losses of two world wars and since suppressed by successive governments of all colours intent only on control and oppression by ever-increasing levels of often incomprehensible legislation.

Many observers in the London area will have seen the dutiful obedience of drivers complying with bus lane legislation despite the fact that this highly polluting means of public transport, the Clapham omnibus was causing congestion by its very nature. With a reserved lane system throughout London choking off the arteries of the capitol for a relatively few subsidised buses and despite the fact that many bus lanes are effective for only a limited number of hours during the day.

Many are familiar with the phrases from the First World War 'keep your head down' and 'never volunteer for anything' and some were only too aware of colleagues who were determined to do as little as possible as employees for the maximum return. Many will recall the likes of the so-called 'red Robbo' Derek Robinson at the Longbridge motor manufacturing plant who brought a large part of Britain's manufacturing industry to its knees. It was all too easy to see why government would wish to allow more enterprising foreign workers into the country in order to undermine the trade unions and the perceived 'lazy' indigenous working population at large. The result of successive governments was arguably to create a compliant, lacklustre, poorly educated largely resentful indigenous if not indolent lower working class population.

Governments had therefore perceived the answer to the many problems they have created eg, the poor state of the economy; to lie in mass immigration which had spiralled totally out of control. By 2019 the indigenous population became passive onlookers to this havoc wreaked about them by incompetent politicians and government whilst in the meantime they continued to fund the ongoing fiascos and largesse of government as if some milking a bottomless pit cash cow.

Following the Second World War tides of immigrants were invited to come to Britain, remember the Windrush; to provide labour for the shortage allegedly caused by the two world wars. By the year 2000 it was evident that mass immigration together with the breeding proclivities of the immigrant population would result in a rapidly expanding more diverse population. By 2010 there is general political agreement that immigration is out of control. It is evident that politicians, renowned for their short-term tactical thinking and ever increasing vacuous promises; are intent on covering up failure to deal with these growing numbers of aliens within the indigenous population. Many first-generation aliens who after some 50 years, in many cases did not yet speak the language of their host country, did not enhance and enrich the indigenous population's way of life as foretold by politicians who had allowed the country to run out of control.

Various attempts at integration and politically correct descriptions have been used to analyse this phenomenon which in 2014 had all the appearance of a deliberate demographic ethnic cleansing policy. Since Enoch Powell's day anyone critical of the situation was described as racist and put down with various unpleasant comments. Descriptions such as 'floods', 'overwhelming', 'swamped', 'damaging to social cohesion' etc were condemned by politicians of all hues in the interest of so-called social cohesion. As the immigrant population grew then so did their influence with politicians all of whom appear to wish to appeal to the middle ground in order to secure the maximum number of votes for the promotion of their own daft ideas and personal careers.

By 2016 most politicians have changed their position and it is now generally agreed that immigration was not only out of control but beyond control, 'the genie and the bottle and/or the elephant in the room'? Despite the Tory government's promises to reduce immigration to tens of thousands by 2015, the date of the election; net immigration continued to increase every year. The UK Independence party (UKIP) saw a rise in its political fortunes whilst the British National Party who had consistently been against immigration see a decline in their political fortunes. 'Tommy Robinson' once leader of the English defence league is rarely heard from as the league sinks into oblivion.

The problem of immigration became a topic 'approved' for discussion albeit it was far too late to do anything about it. As illegal camps of would-be immigrants continue to make their way to the UK and temporarily 'shack up' in Calais, northern France; en route to the UK politicians still appear blind and would not accept that the UK system designed for a 'land fit for heroes' in the late 1940s is undoubtedly the 'pull factor' compelling people to seek a better life, quite often at considerable personal expense, discomfort and sometimes death. The French simply want rid of the problem of desperate young men hanging around Calais.

It is evidently too late by 2020 to do anything meaningful by peaceful means. Politicians wring their hands and make pronouncements whilst living the good life at the expense of their public. They behave in a manner which suggested they were superior to the population at large whilst in reality they appear to be incompetent 'chancers'. It became clear that the politicians who come and go gave no weight to the adverse impact of such rapid social changes eg, mass immigration on the indigenous population who are left to face the consequences created by their ineffective 'leaders' who now wring their hands!

The indigenous population looked on, some with the bemusement, some with disdain but it appears that most looked the other way. The anecdotal research carried out never found anyone within the indigenous population who did not resent the 'imposition' of all those visitors upon them. Are people not entitled to expect their government will protect them from the invasion from aliens? Did the indigenous population have a reasonable expectation that the taxes they were paying was for the benefit of their kith and kin and not for everyone in the whole wide world who may put their hand out? A national not international health service?

The UK was becoming if not already the most diverse country in the world according to Professor David Coleman of Oxford University. Why was this happening? Was it left thinking politicians who had engaged in social manipulation on a grand scale? Was it politicians who had done this to their own population, their own kind in order to 'enrich' society in its diversity? 'God' created a diverse world, he did not create a world where everyone is the same or even equal, he did not create a world where we are all the same in every respect including colour. God created the world where individuals clearly have different attitudes to race, women, the law and much more. Had UK politicians attempted to make everyone conform, look and behave the same through their misguided and idealistic vision of racial integration? Was it God or politicians who created mayhem?

Whilst these debates swirled around the heads of most ordinary people some questioned what it was about the English national mentality that has allowed this. We saw people committed to their country but somewhat docile and compliant. We saw them being policed by a large part of the establishment paid for out of their own taxes in order to maintain a high degree of compliancy. We saw them abused as hosts and mistreated by their guests often with the authorities tacit blessing who appeared to adopt Nelson's blind eye policy.

This compliancy culture was evident from the large numbers in prison for relatively minor offences. When we look back at UK history we can see many signs and indicators as to what has brought us here. The injustices, Timothy Evans, Derek Bentley, Ruth Ellis, Peter Allen and Gwyn Evans whose cases brought hanging to an end The injustices which convicted large numbers of Irish people who had been accused of terrorist bombings on behalf of the IRA and much more. Despite those outrageous injustices, the irreversible nature of capital punishment and the propensity of the British system for gross incompetence it was surprising to see that the population at large nonetheless supported the return of capital punishment if only for certain offences.

The UK population was generally very sympathetic towards the indigenous population of both America and Australia but sympathy is where it ends. We should remember the English were major players in the establishment of the American colonies and discovered Australia. Was the fate of the American Indian and Australian aborigine and later many Arab states an unheeded forecast of the fate of the English and something they should more quickly learned from?

We saw a country inexorably sliding in financial terms with its national debt at approximately £1.5 trillion. We saw a country with a declining military capability and the astonishing argument around the abandonment of the nuclear deterrent on the grounds that it hasn't been necessary so far! The Russians were patrolling the sky of Europe regularly by 2016. How short sighted can it get?

We saw protests on the street by 2017, trade unionists inciting strikes to what purpose? Was there a point to protesting about the inevitable? Let us be clear no one suggested that strikes should be banned but workers using their power to maintain the status quo eg, the British car industry as was; is very short sighted indeed. Is the age of the Luddite still upon us? Without an increase in business activity, productivity and greater exports it was inevitable that further cuts in public services would be made. Was this a bad thing when a large proportion of the country's turnover or GDP, is spent on government activity itself? A pyramid scheme? Nonetheless the riots continued.

Could anyone seriously doubt that the only possible way out of this financial mess was through the mechanics of capitalism and the free market?

Democracy is of course a problem in itself. It gives a vote to the ne'er-do-wells seeking handouts in equal measure if not more so than to those creating wealth. It is clearly politically unacceptable to argue that democratic voting rights should be allocated on a contribution basis. The very idea that one man is worth more or of higher value than another would be politically totally unacceptable. It was inevitable therefore with a growing and significant group demanding more by way of benefits than the taxes paid to support them that the country would continue to become poorer and consequently less able to meet the needs of those making social demands and when increasingly unmet the resultant escalating social unrest.

It was significant that with the publication of the A-level results in 2014 showing a decline in performance and more university places available that standards were destined to fall further leading to a society more willing to resolve problems by force.

It is not difficult to imagine that Iraq, Afghanistan and Syria were better places before the imaginary introduction of so-called Western democracy. With the overthrowing of strong dictators it had been observed that previously secular countries may be subject to a process of Islamification accompanied by a good deal of destruction and violence. We saw significant ancient and long established Christian groups being displaced by the Islamic State in northern Iraq accompanied by the smashing of ancient cultural artefacts. Was this the inevitable fate of Britain?

By 2020 it became of great concern to the indigenous people that democracy appeared to be failing. It appears that mass immigration and the demands from many unable to support themselves drove the country into even greater financial distress and eventually ruin, if it were not already. The evidence suggests that the indigenous population had been written off as lazy, uneconomic and therefore of no benefit to the country. It was short sighted indeed to suggest that the worth of a people is only economic and that there must be some economic payoff from the people; that an ever increasing GDP is paramount. Are a people not entitled to self determination regardless of their economic capitalised value? The country was slow to realise that its own death was far more serious a matter than its perceived economic value alone.

As we are all only too aware the NHS was a huge organisation with over 1 million employees and a political force in its own right. Who could have imagined that such a great idea would inevitably fall into disrepute because of the attitudes and competence of those serving in it. Inevitably it appeared the NHS would become so overwhelmed by the demands placed upon it that it would withdraw into an emergency only service or a pay-as-you-go service. As the English became second class citizens they were often told by their political 'masters', for that is what they saw themselves as; that were it not for immigrants the NHS would collapse.

As greater demands were placed upon the NHS politicians stated that greater funding must be provided to it and that more immigrants are required to fill the vacancies created to service the swelling demand. This sounded like a pyramid selling scheme. The question of who pays for all this was self-evident.

It is very unlikely that anyone is going to deny that people should desire a better life but as in any dynamic system that we may conceive the benefit of one must inevitably be at the disadvantage of another. Such is life for all 7,000,000,000+ inhabitants of the planet the majority of whom live in poor and unpleasant conditions. Competition is as natural a state of affairs to the human condition as are suspicions, hatred and racist feelings.

After the terrible irreversible realisations of reality in 2023 armed gangs openly terrorised London and established no go areas whilst in the North of England women are taken from the streets and outside schools for the pleasure of men who have no stake in society either professionally, ethically or financially.

It appeared inevitable that the country would eventually descend further into anarchy, riots and civil unrest. Those whom the gods wish to destroy, first they make mad! We saw rioting before in our northern cities and more recently in London. These local riots clearly demonstrated the propensity for unrest to easily spread in London and larger cities. They were nothing as compared to the civil war seen in Iraq and Syria. Whilst the English had no desire to fight on their own streets there became a time when they had little choice. There was no democratic solution this time!

Well, if there was no democratic solution. The only possible salvation for Britain was that a strong leader, a dictator; would emerge and take control of the country's resources, infrastructure and armed services. This possible state of affairs appeared attractive, the alternative being anarchy and severe decline. Whilst no one advocated this state of affairs it was the inevitable outcome in a country over which government has little or no real or effective control. The difficulty of course with revolution as we saw in Oliver Cromwell's time, is that the English appear somewhat laissez-faire about their own fate and after establishing a republic for a short time invited back the monarchy in the form of Charles II. Similar events took place in 2026. Whilst the English fought amongst themselves their world was being moved on for them.

In December 2014 Muhammed became the most popular boy's name in the Britain and between 2028 and 2030 we saw England in particular being dominated by the demands of hitherto ethnic minorities with an indigenous population so subdued and docile that no serious attempt is made by them to reassert their obvious rights. The police and army were gradually controlled by ethnic gangs for whom positive discrimination was rampant by way of appeasement. There was eventually fighting in the streets and arguments in Parliament but as politically correct as ever was futile by now. The British Parliament agrees to more ethnic minority MPs who use every opportunity to secure more powers unto themselves. There were no more the likes of Griffin, Robinsons or Cromwells, they had all mysteriously disappeared or retired.

As the result of a combination of short term thinking, political correctness, indifference and incompetence in 2033 we see London, Birmingham, Manchester and Sheffield being controlled completely by armed gangs proclaiming 'Allah Akbar' at every possible opportunity. Public floggings become commonplace. Charles as head of the Church of England is tried in a secret Sharia court, told not to speak and then beheaded publicly. These gangs if only by indifference on the part of the now ineffective police and army both of which are dominated by ethnic factions; oversee the indigenous population living in fear of this aggressive now entrenched 'visitor' to their shores. Not since the Norman conquest has property been sequestrated and redistributed so enthusiastically. Whitehall is divided by territorial gangs who control it from offices in Trafalgar Square and Westminster.

In 2035 we saw the hunting down of non-believers and politicians with the heads of the last three democratically elected prime ministers being stuck on spikes in various public places around Westminster. They have strange looks of disbelief on their contorted faces. There are one or two spirited uprisings by the indigenous population and pockets of resistance continue for some years by those proud of their country's history. Most of the population however for reasons which must be abundantly clear to anyone with eyes to see keep their head down for fear that they may lose it if they do not.

In 2050 we see the country ruled by a President under Sharia law. As Aghia Sophia in Constantinople was converted from a Christian place of worship to an Islamic place of worship before it; Westminster is now the seat of government of the Islamic Republic of Britain. The famous clock tower at the Palace of Westminster now a minaret. All churches now feature at least one minaret and loudspeakers which call the faithful to prayer.

Those who do not attend prayers are questioned and often beaten by the religious police. On Parliament Green there are frequent beheadings and other forms of Sharia punishment carried out by men in loose fitting black clothing and wearing masks. Most have London accents. The statues of Cromwell, Winston Churchill and the rest being long gone. All females are obliged to wear the veil otherwise severe summary punishments are handed out in the street by the same masked men who carry long sticks and the latest powerful assault rifles. Arabic becomes the official language and is broadcast by the successor to the BBC.

It appears that politicians cannot or will not; more importantly the people will not or cannot by any democratic lawful means take control. Elections are suspended indefinitely. The cable TV network is utilised to provide compulsory tele-screens in all homes at the cost of the resident. The tele-screens are two-way communication devices between the authorities and the population and are used to constantly monitor all but the most personal of activities.

Turning off the tele-screens or any damage caused to them is met with severe consequences. Fines are automatically issued to those failing to pray the requisite number of times per day. By 2084 the indigenous population has lost the will to fight or contemplate any other form of positive action such has been their oppression and brainwashing over the last hundred years or so. When a man beats you with a stick it is nice when they stop.

May Allah save us!

As salaam alaikum my brothers and sisters.

The End!

Printed in the United States
By Bookmasters